The Billionaires
of Silicon Forest Prequels

The Gold Digger
The Kiss Catcher
The Game Changer

MELISSA McCLONE

Contents

The Gold Digger

MELISSA McCLONE

Chapter One

"I don't know why I have to see the property this afternoon." Adam Zeile sat next to his friend Henry Davenport in the back of the fully loaded SUV. The windshield wipers worked overtime to clear the torrential downpour. June rainfall was setting records in Oregon. "Hood Hamlet will soon be a flood zone."

"That's why Frank is behind the wheel, not one of us." Henry stretched out his legs. "Trust me. Mother Nature's cry-fest is helping you. The broker says the sellers are eager. The other interested parties are waiting for better weather to view the property."

So that explained why he'd told Adam to drive up to Mount Hood this morning. "You could have mentioned that yesterday."

"It's more fun to hear you complain. Besides, you need a break from work. A Saturday night in Hood Hamlet with me will do you good. If you wind up adding a new property to your portfolio, all the better."

Satisfaction flowed through him. "So, if I want it…"

"Make an offer today, and we'll celebrate tonight."

For a trust fund baby who'd never worked a day in his life and enjoyed spending his money at an alarming rate, Henry had more business sense than most realized.

Adam imagined his dream mountain lodge complete with a helipad. It would be the perfect weekend getaway. He loved living in Portland, but he needed a place where he could relax and not be a quick drive from his company. "Thanks for arranging the showing."

"It's my pleasure. I love spending weekends in Hood Hamlet. Wes Lockhart would live here permanently if he could. Too bad there's not a house for sale on our street."

Adam had stayed with both friends many times over the years. "Your street is great, but I prefer something more secluded."

"Then you'll like this property. The cabin is a teardown, but the location is prime." Henry spoke with confidence. "Main Street will be a quick drive once you pave the road, and you saw the photographs of the view on the listing. It's to die for."

Adam would withhold judgment. "If those photos are an accurate representation."

Henry shook his head. "Have faith."

"Appearances can be deceiving." Adam had been burnt too many times, so he was cautious when it came to business and strangers. He even had his security team run background checks on people he came in contact with, whether for work or pleasure. But that precaution didn't weed out everyone. "And what faith I had disappeared after my last date."

"That bad?"

"She was only interested in my net worth and liquidity. When I didn't want to go out again, she kept calling me. I'm grateful we met at the restaurant. If we'd been alone, she might have made up a story and tried to blackmail me."

Henry cringed. "Ouch."

"The worst part?"

"It gets worse?" Henry joked.

"Ha-ha." Adam leaned his head against the seat. "This has happened three times in a row. The women I meet are all the same—young and attractive with dollar signs in their eyes. There must be a gold digger chat room where they share information about eligible billionaires."

"I'm friends with a lovely matchmaker in San Francisco. I'll ask her if she knows if one exists."

"Be careful. She might be a gold digger herself and lie to you."

"Hadley Lowell is nothing like that." With a narrowed gaze, Henry studied Adam. "Being a billionaire isn't your problem. You just haven't met the right woman."

Adam rolled his eyes. He'd built his successful company based on mathematics and science, not fairy tales and a Magic 8-Ball. "That's because *she* doesn't exist."

"You're wrong because *she* most definitely does. There's someone for everyone. I introduced Brett Matthews to Laurel, and now they have Noelle and are living happily ever after." Henry flashed his phone to show Adam a photo of the little girl. "My goddaughter is the most beautiful child in the world."

For a man who never wanted to settle down, Henry loved Noelle wholeheartedly. "She's cute, but didn't Brett think Laurel was after his money when they got together?"

"That was a huge misunderstanding, which they thankfully resolved."

"Brett got lucky." If there were other women out there like Laurel Worthington Matthews, Adam had never met them. "The other guys have the same problem."

Henry laughed. "Of course, they do. You, Blaise, Dash, Kieran, Mason, and Wes work too much. All of you date women who fall at your feet and won't mind being your lowest priority as long as you provide them with sparkly presents and take them on an occasional expensive outing. You don't want to put in the effort to woo someone, but then you aren't happy when you keep attracting the women who are more interested in your money than in you."

Adam flinched. That hit a little too close to the truth, which was surprising, given Henry's love of partying and serial dating. "You go out with that type."

"I do." Henry didn't hesitate. "The difference is, I want to date those women. The six of you, the so-called Billionaires of Silicon Forest, let them come after you. That's why you end up going out with wannabes and social climbers."

"I'm too busy to pursue someone."

"Most people are, even if they don't have billions."

Adam didn't care about everyone else. He needed to break this pattern so he wouldn't keep being disappointed. "The best thing I can do right now is to take a dating sabbatical."

Henry snorted. "You'll change your mind when we hit the Hood Hamlet Brewing Company tonight."

"I'm serious." Adam raised his chin. "I'm tired of being nothing more than an open wallet to women. I'll just stop dating until I win the 'last single man standing' bet. Then I'll reassess the situation."

Henry rolled his eyes. "I still can't believe you tech geeks made that idiotic bet."

Six of them had put in ten million dollars that would go to the winner—the last one who stayed single. Blaise Mortenson had used a beta investment algorithm he'd created to manage the money. "It's hard to believe that was five years ago."

"Five years and not one of you even has a girlfriend. You're all hopeless." Henry didn't hide his exasperation. "I have an idea. Call off the bet and split the money six ways. Better yet, donate it to worthy charities and take the tax write-off."

"No way." Adam was in it to win it, especially now that he wouldn't be dating. "The fund has grown to almost five hundred million dollars."

Henry's eyes widened. "Impressive, but you can't put a value on true love."

"Love isn't worth half a billion dollars. Not even close."

Laughter lit Henry's hazel-green eyes. "I'll remember you said that."

"Not sure why." But then again, Henry was an eccentric billionaire philanthropist who threw himself ridiculous, over-the-top birthday parties every April Fool's Day and enjoyed meddling in his friends' lives.

"We're almost there," Frank announced. The man was older but a highly skilled driver and bodyguard, which was why Adam had given his security team the weekend off while he stayed with Henry in Hood Hamlet.

"Enjoy seeing the property for the first time," Henry said. "This could be your new home away from home."

Through the rain-streaked windows, Adam glimpsed tall evergreens. He imagined the branches laden with snow come Christmastime. He leaned toward the glass. "Possibly."

"You should be more excited."

Not much excited Adam these days. He hated getting his hopes up only to have them dashed. "I'm optimistic."

"Guess that's better than being full of dread and foreboding. But please be nice to the real estate agent and not a growly, grumpy bear."

His gaze jerked to Henry. "When am I not nice?"

"Your stubbornness can get the best of you at times. And you've been known to go all big brother when one of the guys screws up."

Adam didn't mean to be a grouch, but between work and his friends, he was being pulled in so many directions. While Wes, who was the quintessential big brother of their friend group, went through cancer treatment, Adam had stepped up to take his place. Now that Wes was in remission, Adam should relinquish the title, but he hadn't yet.

Frank turned onto a circular driveway that was more mud than hard-packed dirt. He stopped next to a silver subcompact car and then glanced back. "If we're not here when you finish, text me. Otherwise, we'll return as soon as Henry's done."

"Sorry I forgot about the meeting at the fire station. I would have made the showing for another time," Henry said.

"No problem. If the real estate agent isn't in a hurry, you can check it out when you come back."

"I will." Henry beamed. "But once you see the view from the second story, I have a feeling you'll be sold, and this property will be, too."

"Hope so." Adam unbuckled his seat belt. "See you soon."

He slid out of the SUV, and his feet landed in a puddle. It was a smart move not to wear his best shoes today, but then again, he'd dressed down on purpose. No reason to shout to the real estate agent, or anyone, he would be paying cash. Plus, it was the weekend. No suit or tie for him. He had enough of those during the workweek. Though Henry often dressed as if the Met Gala was an everyday happening in Portland.

Raindrops hit Adam's face. Nothing new on the west side of the Cascades, even in June, but he didn't want to end up too wet. He hurried to the old cabin, dodging more puddles on the way.

He slowed as he reached the covered porch. Not that the roof did much to keep the area dry, especially with water pouring from broken rain gutters.

Definitely a teardown.

But all Adam cared about was the land and the view.

He waved at the SUV before knocking on the purple-painted door.

Let this be the one.

Chapter Two

The door flew open as if the real estate agent had been watching from the dirty front window or heard the car pull up. Adam didn't know if that meant they were in a hurry or eager. Neither boded well.

"Hi." A woman with auburn hair worn in a French twist greeted him with a grin. She bounced as if excited or she needed to use the restroom. "I hope the drive wasn't too bad with this rain. You should come inside so you don't get all wet."

Her words rushed out one on top of the other without her taking any breaths. She motioned him into the cabin, her hands moving as fast as her words had.

As he entered, the unexpected scent of vanilla hit him, reminding him of his mom. If she wasn't baking treats for the family, she was making sachets, potpourri, and candles. But the fragrant smell, the opposite of the decrepit interior, put his suspicions on alert. What was the real estate agent trying to hide?

She closed the door. Her wide smile was pure sunshine

on this overcast day. "I'm Cambria Baker with Portland Rose Realty."

"I'm Adam Zeile."

"It's so nice to meet you." She extended her arm.

His fingers touched hers, and a spark flashed.

He jerked his hand away.

"Oh, sorry." As a blush rushed from her neck to her face, Cambria shook out her hand and then grinned. "The carpet must hold a charge or something."

Or something was his guess. She was here to show him the cabin, but had she known who he was, or Henry who'd made the appointment? If that were the case, she might try to convince Adam of a spark—chemistry—between them.

Call him paranoid, but his trust had to be earned.

She smiled at him. "This place is a lot to take in."

So was she. Cambria Baker was younger than he expected—mid-twenties, perhaps. She was also beautiful with high cheekbones, bright green eyes, and full lips. If he went for that type. Once, he had. Okay, as of last weekend, he had.

But no longer.

No matter what Henry thought, Adam was serious about not dating. He needed to focus on buying land and winning the bet. Nothing else. "Are you the listing broker?"

"Heavens no. I haven't been in real estate long enough for that." Cambria rubbed her hands together as if she were cold—or nervous. Nerves might explain why she practically buzzed with frenetic energy. "My broker asked me to do the showing for her. I, um, hope that's okay."

No, it wasn't, because this woman had too much in common with his recent dates. Granted, he'd known her for less than sixty seconds, so he might be hypercritical based on his experiences. Adam studied her.

Her skirt and blazer fit loosely as if they were at least a size too big. The professional style was acceptable for a real estate showing in Portland, but she wasn't dressed for a rainstorm on Mount Hood. Somehow, her hair and makeup were perfect despite the constant rain falling from the sky. Her pumps, too.

Everything about her shouted, "trying too hard."

His muscles tensed. Henry wanted him to be nice, but each nerve ending stood on alert. The fight-or-flight instinct kicked in because Adam had no idea how far Cambria would go to get a sale.

Or something else.

Adam fought the urge to run out the door. Two things stopped him—the rain and no car. Hood Hamlet was too far to walk, especially in the wet weather, and he still hadn't seen the view from the second story.

A voice sounded.

Oops. She'd been telling him about the cabin, but he hadn't been paying attention.

"Nothing has been updated for years." She pointed at the dark faux wood paneling. "But if you can look past the avocado-green and harvest-gold décor, you'll recognize the unlimited potential, as a flip-house, an investment, remodel, or a teardown. There are pros and cons to each, but the possibilities are endless with a little imagination and elbow grease."

As she headed into the kitchen, he followed, noticing the bounce to her step. She couldn't be this excited or nervous all the time. A person would get exhausted trying to be "on" that much. Maybe she saw a different kind of dollar sign—sales commission—and that explained her vivaciousness.

"The cabin belongs to a large family. For decades, grandparents, their children, and the new generation used it. I can imagine how much love and laughter filled these walls." Her spiel sounded rehearsed and a tad over the top, but he conceded this was part of her job no matter who was a potential buyer. "But as everyone grew older, they no longer had time to spend here. Since then, it's been used as a vacation rental for ski teams and groups, which explains the wear and tear."

That was one way to put it. Disgusting was another. Everything was dated and not kitschy or hip retro. But since this was a teardown, the condition didn't matter.

She motioned to a plate of cookies, tea bags, instant coffee packets, mugs, a thermal carafe, and water bottles on the olive-green Formica countertop. "Before I show you more, I have refreshments if you're hungry or thirsty."

The cookies—chocolate chip—appeared to be homemade. Next to them lay an exclusive buyer service agreement, her business card, and a pen.

Confident or presumptuous? Or just trying to do her job?

"Please, help yourself." She raised the plate toward him. "I made the cookies."

Adam took a step back. "No, thanks."

She sucked in a breath but said nothing. As she returned the plate to the counter, he noticed a vanilla candle flickering nearby. That explained the smell in the cabin. Was Cambria's cheerfulness as fake as the scent?

A valid question because no one's smile was that bright or unwavering, especially when he wasn't the most polite client. Although, she was a salesperson, so maybe she followed the adage "the customer was always right."

Cambria bit her lip. "Would you like something to drink?"

Next, she would hand him her card and ask him to sign her agreement. Adam wasn't ready to do that. "Could I see the second floor? I want to check out the view."

"Oh, for sure. That's the biggest selling point of this property. I just love it so much, and you will, too. Please, follow me." Her singsong voice belonged in a kindergarten classroom. "There are a few leaks from the rain, so watch where you step or you might land in a puddle."

Too late for that, but he appreciated the warning.

As he followed her up the creaking stairs, he ignored the sway of her hips.

Dating hiatus, he reminded himself.

The condition of the upstairs was worse than the first floor. He found it difficult to believe people paid to stay here.

She motioned to an open door. "The clouds are in the way, so you may need to use your imagination to fill in the details, but this bedroom has the best view."

Adam stood at the large window. This must be where someone took the photograph on the listing because the angle was similar. Rainy weather aside, the view was gorgeous. He imagined a sunny bluebird day. Yes, the reality lived up to what he'd seen on the internet. Except, something felt…off. He couldn't explain it, but he trusted his gut, which told him, "No, this isn't it."

That sucked because it meant his search had to continue. At this rate, he wouldn't be spending a white Christmas in his vacation home.

A text notification sounded. He glanced at his phone.

Henry: *Meeting canceled. Flood warning. We're on our way to you.*
Adam: *Drive safe.*
Henry: *How's the view?*
Adam: *I'll tell you when you get here.*

"I've seen enough." Adam tucked his phone into his pocket. "My friend is picking me up. The area is under a flood warning. Are you from Hood Hamlet?"

"Portland."

That meant she had an hour-plus drive ahead of her. Maybe longer with the pouring rain. At least it was daylight. "You should get home as soon as you can."

With that, he headed downstairs.

She followed him. "Do you mind if I clean up while you wait for your ride?"

"Do whatever you have to do so you can get out of here."

Something—desperation, perhaps—gleamed in her eyes. "Are you interested in the property?"

"No." He didn't believe in wasting anyone's time or raising their hopes. "The view is stunning, but something doesn't feel right."

Her face fell before her expression became neutral. "I understand. You'll know when it's the perfect place for you. If you aren't working with a real estate agent, I'd be happy to help you find the property you want."

She said the correct words, but the bubbliness—the eagerness—from before was missing. He wanted to hug her until she smiled again, which made no sense. But her disappointment was palpable, and he wanted to tell her it wasn't personal. She might have rubbed him the wrong way, but that wasn't why he didn't like the property.

"I don't know what my next step will be." That was the truth, but the way she stared at the carpet, almost curling into herself, made him want to buy the place just so she wouldn't look so sad. "Clean up so you can get out of here. I'll wait by the front door. Thank you for showing me the cabin."

There. Adam had been polite. He hoped that was enough for Henry.

Her gaze bounced from the form to her business card he hadn't picked up. What light remained in her eyes dimmed. "You're welcome. I hope you find what you're looking for."

As Adam went to the entryway, he felt like a jerk for not taking her card, but he appreciated she hadn't pushed him to sign the agreement or call her.

A few minutes later, Cambria came toward him. She'd changed into black leggings, an oversized gray hoodie, and rain boots. One large tote bag hung off her shoulder, and she carried another.

Her new outfit explained how she'd stayed clean and dry, but these clothes made her appear younger. The sadness in her eyes gave her an air of vulnerability that was difficult to ignore.

A protectiveness welled up inside him, which was odd when he was the one who'd made her feel bad. The least he could do was not make her wait.

"Go ahead and lock up the cabin." He was still damp from when he arrived. A little more rain wouldn't hurt him. "I'll wait outside."

Her forehead wrinkled. "Listen to the rain. It's pouring again. You'll get soaked out there."

"My friend will be here soon," he countered. "You should get on the road, given the weather."

An uncomfortable silence descended.

Come on, Henry. Adam shifted his weight between his feet.

A noise sounded.

Henry and Frank must be here. Adam blew out a breath before opening the door, but no SUV was parked next to the other car.

Rain pelted the ground, and water poured like a sheet from the roof. But the noise he'd heard became louder—rumbled.

Her face paled.

Adrenaline surged. "Earthquake?"

"Slide." Cambria pushed him aside, slammed the door, and grabbed his hand with her free one. "Upstairs!"

The rumble turned into a roar—deafening and frightening and all-consuming.

The bag on her shoulder swung and nearly took him out, but he stayed upright.

As she ran up the stairs and into the bathroom, she never let go of him. "Get in the tub."

Adam's pulse raced. He shouldn't be winded, but his breaths came fast. "Isn't that for a tornado?"

Cambria released his hand and climbed into the bathtub. She flashed him a stop-being-ridiculous look.

The rumbling continued.

He didn't need to be told twice and got in next to her.

"We should be safe here," she reassured him.

Something crashed into the house with an earsplitting blast. The cabin shook.

She gasped.

Adam bounced against the wall and then fell. He held back a shout.

Cambria curled in a ball, so he covered her with his body. He had no idea what was happening, and he wasn't sure if he wanted to know.

His heart pounded, threatening to explode, but that didn't drown out the horrible sounds of breaking glass and splintering wood.

Is this how it ends?

He imagined his mom, dad, brother, and sister. A carousel of his friends followed.

Adam gulped in air as if it might be his last breath. Images of the future he wouldn't have filled his mind—a wife, kids, and a forever kind of love.

"I think it's over," a quiet voice said from underneath him.

He straightened so that Cambria could sit up.

She was correct. Everything had stopped, but he had no sense of time or how long they'd been in the bathroom.

Her face was paler than before. Her lower lip quivered.

Adam touched her shoulder. "It'll be okay."

She raised an eyebrow. "And you know this how?"

Her sarcastic tone surprised him.

"I don't." Tired of cowering, he stood and found his footing in the tub. "But we're alive. I wasn't sure if we would be by the time everything stopped. And you look like you needed to hear it."

She didn't disagree. Nor did she say anything.

"Thanks for getting me upstairs. I had no idea what was happening." Adam didn't know the extent of damage on the first floor, but he assumed—hoped—the immediate danger had passed. "How did you know to run upstairs?"

"My grandpa was on our neighborhood's Community Emergency Response Team. He stopped when he and my grandma moved into an assisted living center, but now he's the head of the CERT he formed there. He taught my brother and me what to do in different, um, situations."

Her voice shook, and her hands trembled.

Was she afraid or in shock? Perhaps both?

Adam hadn't taken a first aid class in years. His security team included a medic, so he hadn't needed to remember anything and didn't. "You okay?"

She nodded. "Delayed reaction."

That was a relief.

"You should check on your friend," she added.

Henry and Frank.

Adam's heart dropped. As he yanked out his phone and hit call, he held his breath.

One ring. Two…

"Are you okay?" Henry asked in a breathless rush.

Tears pricked the back of Adam's eyelids. He exhaled, letting his tension go, and cleared his throat. "If by okay you mean standing in the bathtub on the second floor, then yes, I'm okay. What about you and Frank?"

"If we'd been two minutes earlier, we would have been caught in the mudslide."

"Mudslide," Adam repeated so Cambria would know she'd been correct. Not that he'd doubted her. She'd taken action while he stood frozen, unable to make sense of what was happening. "Something hit the house, but we haven't been downstairs to see what. How bad is it where you are?"

"The road is covered with mud. There's no way to pick you up."

Adam let the news sink in. "But you and Frank—"

"We're fine."

He needed to hear that again. "How long do you think cleanup will take?"

"Frank is on the phone with someone. But I doubt it'll be fast. With this weather, calling in a helicopter isn't an option."

That meant… Adam scrubbed his face. "So, I'm stuck."

"Yes, but at least you're not alone."

He glanced at Cambria, whose arms wrapped around her knees. She'd bitten off her lipstick and had a faraway look in her eyes.

"Will you be okay if you have to stay the night there?" Henry asked.

"I have no idea what the mud did to the house, but do I have a choice?"

"Not at the moment. I'll call or text when I know more." In the background, Frank mumbled something. "Don't waste your cell phone battery in case there's no power."

The bathroom's light wasn't on, but Adam couldn't remember if it had been before.

"I won't." Even if they had electricity, it wouldn't matter because his charger was sitting in his bag at Henry's place. "And please, do what you can to get me out of here."

Chapter Three

So, I'm stuck.

Mr. Zeile's annoyed words echoed through Cambria's head, but they didn't quite register. Not while her insides trembled, her heart beat in quadruple time, and tears threatened to fall. She'd held herself together through his not wanting the property, being rejected as his future agent, and then finding herself in a real-life version of a bad direct-to-cable disaster flick.

And now, she struggled not to lose it.

Because that would be big-time ugly.

Sure, when the mudslide began, Cambria had been the plucky heroine whose years of training kicked in, propelling her into action, but she'd had no idea what would happen after she climbed into the tub. Denial, most likely because when the house shook and Adam covered her, fear had seized her. She'd never been so grateful to have someone with her.

She'd expected her life to flash before her eyes. Except, it hadn't, which made her wonder how a dead person could relay to anyone living what occurred during their last few seconds on this earth. To be honest, she didn't have much to look back on, but those few memories, including the bad ones, would have been easier to handle than the all-consuming worry about her grandma and grandpa. Her death would destroy them emotionally and financially.

A lump burned in Cambria's throat.

Why have I never considered buying life insurance?

Okay, she was twenty-four and healthy, but not immortal. Accidents, illnesses, natural disasters killed people her age and younger every single day. Yet, not once had she thought about making sure her grandparents would be okay if something happened to her.

Ugh.

Her grandparents relied on her help to pay for their apartment at the assisted living center. If she died, they would lose their only granddaughter, which would suck big-time, but also the place where they lived. It had been hard enough for Cambria to get them into an affordable, decent facility. They wouldn't be able to do that again on their own, and her brother, Beck, would never return from Las Vegas to Portland.

She'd already asked if he would, and he'd said no.

When Cambria got home, she would research and apply for term life insurance. Somehow she would find the money to cover the premiums. Though she had no idea how much that would cost.

Mr. Zeile put his phone into his pocket and crossed his arms over his chest. If he meant to appear menacing, he'd succeeded.

Cambria should be intimidated, but perhaps being near death, if only in her mind, made a person stronger…or pluckier. "Is your friend okay?"

"Yes, but he said the mudslide blocked the road."

His stormy blue eyes matched the frustration on his face. Tall with handsome features, styled brown hair, and a neatly trimmed beard, he was probably in his early thirties. The way his jeans, a long-sleeved T-shirt, and a zip-up rain jacket fit told her he worked out, but his hands were smooth, not calloused or scarred. His manicured and clean nails suggested he didn't do manual labor. He probably had a good job to be able to afford to buy a cabin or land or whatever he wanted.

Attractive, yes, but his better-than-you personality, and lips that appeared immune to smiles were complete turnoffs. No amount of gorgeous would make up for his rudeness, though he didn't seem to be a total beast. She appreciated him protecting her when whatever crashed into the house hit.

He rubbed his neck. "We won't be able to leave until that's cleared."

That meant they both were trapped, but it shouldn't be for long.

As she stood, one bag hung haphazardly from her shoulder. The other tote lay at her feet. The top of her head came to the tip of his nose. She raised her chin, but that didn't give her any more height. "An hour will go by fast."

His mouth slanted. "It might be longer than that."

Uh-oh. Cambria inhaled sharply. She had to be in Portland tonight. The showing had been at one o'clock, giving her plenty of time to drive back to town—until the mudslide.

She cleared her dry throat. "Did your friend say how long it'll be until we can leave?"

He eyed her warily, the way he'd been doing since they met at the cabin's front door.

What was his problem? She'd done her job: driven up in the rain, spruced up the place, lit a scented candle, offered him refreshments, and showed him a spectacular view. He'd looked for less than two minutes, not only wasting her time but also putting them in this situation.

"My friend will find out, but he thought we might be here overnight," he said.

Overnight.

The word reverberated through her like a death knell. Suddenly, life insurance was no longer her biggest concern. Being stuck here that long would mean missing shifts at two jobs, not to mention the open house she was hosting for someone else tomorrow.

Tears pricked her eyes. She blinked, forcing herself not to look upward where he stood.

Do. Not. Cry.

Cambria had to hold herself together. Mr. Zeile wanted nothing to do with the property or her, but she represented the real estate company. She needed to be professional, even if her world was about to implode.

"Are you okay?" he asked.

"That's… It can't take that long." Her voice sounded shrill, but being on the verge of panic did that to a person.

There would be no sales commission coming this month, nor a referral fee from another agent. Cambria's share of her grandparents' July rent sat in her checking account, waiting to be automatically deducted by the facility. August's payment, however, would be impossible for her to make if she lost one or both of her jobs that paid hourly. "I have to be in Portland by six o'clock tonight."

He raised a brow. "Hot date?"

His question didn't deserve an answer, so she ignored him. He had to be wrong about the road.

W-R-O-N-G.

The alternative was…unthinkable.

She would be there on time. Somehow. Some way.

Cambria grabbed the bag at her feet and climbed out of the tub.

Mr. Zeile stared at her as if she were a piece of gum stuck on the bottom of his shoe. "Where are you going?"

"Downstairs to see what happened and if there's a way out."

"It may not be safe."

She didn't know why he cared. His expression, his mannerisms, and his tone had told Cambria he disliked her on sight. Still, he was right. She had no idea what she might find and didn't need to carry the bags with her. She placed them on the linoleum floor and got her phone.

"I'll be careful." Her voice sounded strong, given the situation.

He said nothing, but a vein pulsed at his jaw. Okay, the man didn't talk much. Some people preferred to let their actions speak, but this guy took it to a new level.

"Be back soon." She didn't know why she told him anything, especially when he didn't respond.

Cambria headed down the stairs carefully. One creaked. Another cracked. That was no different from when they'd used them before. As she descended, the smell changed. The temperature dropped. She shivered.

On the first floor, mud was everywhere.

The sliding glass doors had shattered. A gaping hole in the kitchen allowed rain to blow into the house. A tree lay on top of the island while a gas grill and patio furniture were on their sides.

"Oh, boy." Thank goodness they hadn't stayed downstairs.

Cambria trudged through the mud, careful to place one foot before moving the other to keep from falling on something she couldn't see. Her boots kept her feet dry, but mud covered them. Thankfully, the flow had stopped halfway into the living room so she could—and did—open the door.

Her car sat where she'd left it and appeared fine.

She blew out a relieved breath. *Thank you.*

That car would save her from living on the streets at the end of the month.

Rain fell, but it was lighter than earlier. She went outside.

As she continued down the driveway, she froze at the disaster in front of her. Mud and debris covered everything, much worse than in the house. A glance uphill showed the path of the slide and how lucky they'd been. If the house had been closer to the road, the mud would have swept it away with them inside.

Still, her heart dropped.

Mr. Zeile's friend was correct. No way would she be in Portland tonight. They might be stuck here overnight, if not longer.

The realization weighed heavily on Cambria. Her shoulders sagged.

No!

She needed to be proactive, not throw herself a pity party. That meant doing everything in her power to save her jobs—all three of them. Not for herself, but her grandparents.

On her way back to the cabin, she called Lycaon, the restaurant where she washed dishes, and explained the situation to the lunch hostess, who promised to tell the manager. Next, she contacted the bakery where she worked the early shift on Sundays, but no one answered. She left a message about being stuck in Hood Hamlet. Then, she texted her broker about being trapped by the mudslide and how that might affect Cambria hosting tomorrow's open house.

Not that it would matter. She'd been a real estate agent for three months and hadn't landed a client or made a sale.

The worst real estate agent in the state of Oregon.

The other agents at the office jokingly called her that, and she was living up to the title today.

With the calls completed, she had only one thing left to do—make Mr. Zeile comfortable for however long it took until they could leave. Her car was locked and her keys upstairs, so she would need to make another trip out here to get food and water for them. If she focused on taking care of Mr. Zeile, she wouldn't obsess over the worst-case scenarios happening. She went inside.

When Cambria reached the staircase, she climbed two steps, removed her muddy boots, and left them there. The bathroom where they'd been was empty, so she grabbed her bags and followed the sound of a male voice talking in one of the bedrooms.

"I appreciate the help, Wes." Mr. Zeile had his back to her and his phone at his ear. "I just want to go home."

Cambria's sock-covered feet made no noise, so she pushed open the door until it banged against the wall.

"Talk to you soon." As he lowered the phone, he faced her. "How bad is it?"

"We were lucky. The kitchen and dining area took the biggest hit. It's probably safer if we stay upstairs."

He glanced at her feet. "Did you go outside?"

"Yes." She placed her two bags and the phone on the bed. "The front is fine, but the closer you get to the road, the worse it gets. I'm not sure the road is still there."

"The electricity is out." His Adam's apple bobbed. He jiggled his phone. "Not that I brought my charge cord with me."

She studied his cell phone—top of the line. "Mine is the same brand, but an older model. I have two portable chargers with me if your battery is dying."

His eyebrow rose again. "Two?"

"I'm rarely home, so they come in handy when I'm out." She pulled one from her purse, plugged in the charging adaptor, and handed it to him. "Use this, Mr. Zeile."

"Thanks, but call me Adam." His blue-eyed gaze met hers.

Her heart bumped.

The shared glance unnerved her more than the shock she'd felt earlier when they shook hands. Something about him unsettled her. She rubbed her clammy palms against her leggings.

"I'm Cambria, but you know that." She removed items from the first bag: a container of cookies, water bottles, tea, coffee, the carafe. "I thought I'd inventory our supplies, in case we need to ration them."

"Good idea, but between the sugar and caffeine, we'll be up all night, so you might want to factor that into your plan."

She couldn't tell if he was making a joke. "I have more food in my car."

He held his hands up, palms facing her. "Hey, I'm not complaining. I only have my wallet and phone. Those won't help me much."

"That's okay." The words rushed out. She didn't like how he made her nervous. "I have enough for both of us."

"Of course, you do." He eyed the items on the bed before staring at her. "You're the one with the training. What should we do next?"

They had plenty of daylight left, but she didn't want to waste any. "I need to grab my keys and get things out of my car."

"Do you want help?"

Yes. "No, um, but thanks. You don't have boots."

"I've never let a little dirt or mud stop me."

Funny. He sounded almost flirty. But that wasn't possible.

"Check the closets and drawers in here. See if there's anything useful like a flashlight or blankets. When I get back, we can split up the rest of the rooms. If you need me, just yell." *Oh, no.* She was rambling. "Not me. Help. My help, I mean."

A smile tugged at his lips. "I know what you mean."

As her stomach fluttered, she dug out her keys from her purse and bolted out of the bedroom.

Ugh. Why did being around him turn her into a babbling idiot?

Chapter Four

As Adam opened the middle drawer in the dresser, he laughed at his situation. Once the weather cleared, he would pay for a helicopter to rescue him, if Blaise's wasn't available, but until then, his money was worthless. No one could reach him by land. Not today, possibly not tomorrow. He was completely reliant on items the cabin's owners had left behind and whatever the real estate agent had brought with her.

I have enough for both of us.

He'd assumed Cambria wanted something from him, but she was willing to share what she had with him.

Ironic.

Wes, whose advice had become more sage since his cancer treatments, would tell Adam there was a lesson to learn here.

Probably.

Nothing was in the drawer, so he opened the bottom one.

Adam was grateful for Cambria's preparedness. He

would have never thought of carrying portable power charges and extra food with him.

Who was he kidding?

He never had to do anything for himself. Someone— okay, multiple people—took care of whatever he needed: meals, groceries, toiletries, clean clothes, a spotless house, reservations when he wanted to eat out. A person even detailed his cars and kept them full of gas without him asking. He couldn't remember the last time he'd cooked for himself other than heating leftovers in the microwave.

Now stuck in a cabin, Cambria was making sure he had food, even after he'd made a snap judgment, lumping her in with the gold diggers he'd dated, and allowing that opinion to influence his actions. As guilt coated his mouth, Adam hung his head. He didn't deserve her kindness or generosity, but he would accept it.

The truth was, he had no idea who Cambria Baker was beyond being a real estate agent. She could be a gold digger, but she might also be someone overly enthusiastic about her job. The woman mystified him, and like a brain teaser that needed to be solved, Adam wanted to piece together the parts.

No matter how competent and take-charge she appeared to be, vulnerability and fear occasionally flashed like neon signs on Cambria's face. Ever since the mudslide, she'd teetered on the edge of a tightrope. He kept waiting for her to lose it, but somehow, she held herself together.

Adam wasn't sure whether to be impressed or to tell her to have an ugly cry and get out her emotions. That was what his mom suggested he and his siblings do when strong feelings hit. Maybe if he found something useful, it would take the pressure off her or just make her smile.

He sorted through filled-in Yahtzee scoresheets and brochures to the local tourist sites and activities on Mount Hood. Those were worthless unless they needed kindling, but the fireplace was downstairs, and that should remain unlit.

After closing the drawer, Adam checked the closet. Only one thing caught his eye—a wool blanket on the top shelf. Not exactly a treasure, but if the temperature dropped, that could keep them warm. He added it to the stuff on the bed. Now, to find more…

A phone rang, shattering the quiet. The ringtone, however, wasn't his.

Cambria's cell phone lay on the bed. He had no idea if she'd called for help while she'd been downstairs, so he answered. "Cambria Baker's phone."

"H-hello," a man replied, sounding unsure. "Is this Beck?"

"No." But Adam was curious if one of the two men was her boyfriend.

"Oh, okay." The guy sounded disappointed. "Is Cambria there?"

"She's getting something from her car. Can I take a message?"

"Yes, this is Sam Owens, her next-door neighbor. I'm about to head to the airport on vacation."

So, not her hot date. Adam smiled, though he didn't

understand why he cared.

"Please tell her I put boxes on her patio and covered them with a tarp," Sam continued. "She can keep that to hide the stuff she has to leave in her car."

What her neighbor said made no sense, but it didn't matter. "I'll relay the message."

"Thanks." Silence filled the line. "It's such a shame what's happening to her. Family shouldn't do that to each other."

Once again, Adam had no clue what Sam meant, but it sounded as if he thought a family member had mistreated Cambria.

"Our landlord is so upset about evicting her. It's not often you see a grown man sob, and Cambria stepped right up to comfort him." Sam exhaled loudly. "But that's who she is. Always looking out for others, especially her grandparents. She's good people."

"Good people," Adam repeated without even thinking because he'd seen that side of her today. Except, a person didn't get evicted without a reason—such as not paying rent or breaking the rules. He wondered what Cambria had done and why the landlord had cried.

"Has she found a place to stay?" Sam asked.

"No idea." Which was the truth.

Sam laughed. "Sounds like she doesn't tell you much, either. Typical Cambria."

Did that mean she was secretive or private? Maybe both?

Stop. Adam needed to stop judging people.

"Have you talked her out of living in her car?" Sam asked.

The question slammed into Adam.

Eviction. Living in her car. The tarp.

As images formed in his mind, he gripped the phone. "No."

"I gave up, but I'll text links to places that can help her. Tell her to reach out to them before she moves out."

Into her car? Adam's throat tightened. "I will."

The man said goodbye and disconnected from the call.

A text notification sounded, followed by four more.

Adam shouldn't read them, but he wanted—needed—to know more.

Mr. O: *https://ugmportland.org/*
Mr. O: *https://www.tprojects.org*
Mr. O: *https://rosehaven.org/*
Mr. O: *https://humansolutions.org*
Mr. O: *https://www.catholiccharitiesoregon.org*

Adam's breath hitched. He recognized the URLs—organizations in Portland that helped people in need. The fact Cambria would have to reach out to any of them floored him—made his gut churn.

That was…

Unexpected.

But that adjective appeared to best describe Cambria Baker.

He returned her phone to the bed and tried to figure out what kind of trouble she was in, because no matter what a person did for a living, an eviction was a big problem.

His gut instinct about her wanting money had been correct, but he might have been wrong about her motivations. Now the way her clothes had hung on her made more sense. So did the food she'd set out for him—tea bags, instant coffee, and homemade cookies, not a coffee traveler from Starbucks and store-bought treats.

Cambria trying so hard during the showing most likely had nothing to do with her being a gold digger, but everything to do with the situation she found herself in and the need to make a sale. If so, he was a complete jerk for the way he'd acted toward her, especially considering how she'd kept her cool during the mudslide and gotten them both to safety.

But that's who she is.

According to Sam, yes, but Adam knew little about her. He wanted to change that. She'd helped him—was still helping him—and he hoped to do the same for her.

"I can't reach the kitchen cabinets, but we should have enough food to last two, maybe three, days." Cambria entered the room. She held a case of water bottles with a box sitting on top. She placed both on the bed. "Oh, a blanket. Great find."

"It was in the closet." He glanced at her phone. "Your neighbor Sam called."

Worry clouded her gaze. "He's leaving on his vacation today. Is he okay?"

Her concern appeared genuine. Another data point for her being "good people."

"He's fine. He left boxes on your patio. He said to keep

the tarp and use it to cover things in your car."

Her cheeks reddened. "Oh, thanks. I'm, uh, moving out of my apartment, so Sam gave me some boxes. And I guess a tarp."

"Nice of him."

"Yes. I'll miss him when I leave." The words rushed out.

Adam waited for her to say more, but she didn't. "Sam is texting links for places."

"Thanks." Cambria grabbed her phone. As she studied the screen, she bit her lip.

He fought the urge to move closer. "Everything okay?"

Her gaze jerked up to meet his. "Yes, everything is fine."

The way her words came out almost on top of each other suggested otherwise. Her situation was none of Adam's business, yet he wanted to help her.

She typed on her screen before slipping her phone into her hoodie pocket. "Now it's time to see what else we can find. Ready?"

He was ready to find out more about her, but a scavenger hunt would have to do for now. "Yes."

"You search the rooms on the right. I'll take the left side. We'll meet back here to inventory everything." She headed out the door before he could reply.

In the next bedroom, he found nothing in the closet or dresser. That left the armoire. But first, he sent a text to Dash Cabot, a friend nicknamed Wonderkid because of his brilliant mind and his age. He was the youngest of their group. He was also a master hacker.

Adam: *Hey, stuck because of a mudslide. Can you look into Cambria Baker for me? She's a real estate agent with Portland Rose Realty.*
Dash: *Henry told us what happened on the group chat. Glad you're okay. Is she the woman trapped with you?*
Adam: *Yes.*
Dash: *Another gold digger?*
Adam: *I don't know.*
Dash: *I'll find out what I can.*
Adam: *Thanks.*

He opened the armoire, empty except for board games and puzzles on the top shelf. The boxes were old and a few torn, but these would give them something to do while they waited for the road to be cleared or help to arrive.

With his arms loaded, Adam returned to the other bedroom and put his finds on the dresser.

"Oh, wow." Cambria sounded excited. "You found better stuff than me."

"Your food and water top everything."

"Wait until you see what I have before saying that." She pulled out instant noodle cups, tuna, saltine crackers, squeezable apple sauce, granola bars, and pretzels. "More savory than sweet, but we have the cookies, too."

Her "we" sent warmth pooling in his chest. *Weird.*

Adam focused on the food. Most of the brands were generic and not the most nutritious items, but they wouldn't go hungry. "Definitely tops."

Her grin brightened her face—the result, breathtaking. "Thanks."

"Do you normally have that much food in your car?"

She nodded. "I'm out most of the day. This way, I don't have to pack a lunch or eat out. That would be too expensive."

Adam ate out most of the time, but then again, he could afford to. "Real estate keeps you busy?"

She nodded. "Plus, there's other stuff I do."

That piqued his interest. "Such as?"

Cambria shrugged. "You really want to know?"

"Yes."

She organized the food into piles. "Real estate is all commission, and it's been difficult to establish myself, so I'm working other jobs for now."

The plural wasn't lost on him. "You mentioned you hadn't been in real estate long."

"A few months, but I'll get there." She picked up a granola bar. "Hungry?"

"No."

"How does playing a board game or putting together a puzzle sound?" she asked.

It wasn't as if he had much to do except be on his phone. And maybe he could find out more about her this way. "Sure."

"Sorry?"

Her apologizing made no sense. "What are you sorry for?"

Cambria laughed. "I meant the game. Do you want to play Sorry?"

Oh, right. "Okay."

She practically bounced as she picked up the box from the dresser. "Beck and I played this all the time with my grandparents."

Sam had mentioned that name. "Is Beck your boyfriend?"

Another laugh. She sat on the floor and set up the board. "He's my brother."

"Good."

A V formed between her eyebrows. "Why good?"

Uh-oh. Adam hadn't realized what he said…or why. But he had to answer her question.

"It's good you have those memories." That wasn't a total save, but a decent enough answer. He sat across from her, curious if she bought it. "Are you close to your brother?"

"We used to be thick as thieves." The light in her eyes dimmed. "We shared an apartment with his best friend, Hunter, but they moved to Las Vegas in March. More opportunity there."

She sounded so dejected. Adam wanted to know why. "Are you moving because they left?"

Cambria nodded. "I like the apartment complex, but the place is way too big for me by myself. I tried to find roommates, but I didn't have much luck."

Her brother must be the family Sam mentioned. If the two left Cambria with a lease she couldn't afford, that would explain the eviction. "What does your brother do?"

"Construction. He flips houses." She set out the game pieces. "He planned on starting his business here, which is why I got my real estate license, but the housing prices were too high, so he and Hunter moved there. They love it and have plenty of work. And Beck has a girlfriend now."

Cambria said all the right words, but her bubbliness was gone. "You miss him."

She nodded, not raising her gaze from the board. "It's been…different since he left."

Different or difficult? Adam guessed the latter. "Did you consider going to Las Vegas with him?"

"No, because our grandparents live in Portland." As she spoke, she rubbed her thumb over a game piece. "Beck asked them if they'd move, and they said no, so I stayed. I would never leave them alone. That would be… Wrong. So very wrong."

Her earnest tone struck him as genuine. It appeared Sam was correct about Cambria, and Adam needed to stop making snap judgments. "Your grandparents are lucky to have you."

"Oh, no. I'm the lucky one." She placed each of her game pieces in the starting spots. "They took my brother and me in when no one else wanted us. Without them, who knows where we'd be? I owe them everything."

What about Beck? But Adam didn't ask. The affection and gratitude in her voice matched the gleam in her eyes. "Then, you're fortunate to have each other."

She nodded. "So, what do you do?"

Saying he was the CEO and chairman of the board of a multibillion-dollar company might be accurate, but he usually went with something less specific. "Hi-tech stuff."

"In an office?"

He preferred calling their brand-new corporate headquarters a state-of-the-art campus. "Yes."

"So, you know about business?"

He nodded. "Do you have a question about something?"

Her gaze met his, unfurling something in his stomach.

She leaned forward. "How expensive is term life insurance?"

That was not what he expected to hear. He swallowed a laugh until he remembered her situation. "It depends on your definition of expensive, but you're young. Why do you need life insurance?"

She sighed. "It's because of my grandparents. I'm all they've got, and if something happened to me, they wouldn't be able to afford where they live."

Chapter Five

"I win!"

Cambria shimmied her shoulders, excited because she'd never played this well with her family. Adam must be her new good luck charm. She sure needed one.

"Again," she added for effect.

He groaned. "You had to rub it in."

"It's not every day I win four times in a row," she teased.

They'd spent hours playing and talking. Whatever had caused his earlier dislike of her no longer seemed to be an issue. That made her happy because she enjoyed his company. He was funny, smart, and attractive. She was always up for appreciating eye candy.

He rubbed his beard. "Statistically—"

"It happened, and math should be illegal on weekends."

As she put away the game pieces, her fingers brushed his. No spark this time, but tingles spread outward from the point of contact. His sharp inhale suggested he felt something, too. Or, she might be allowing her imagination to get the best of her. "I've got it."

"You've been taking care of everything, including me."

"Occupational hazard since I was the one showing you the cabin."

His gaze locked on hers. "I appreciate all you've done, Cambria."

Her breath stilled. "You're welcome."

"The least I can do is help put away the game."

"Okay." Cambria forced the word from her dry throat and then focused on the board, but she was hyper-aware of him—his movements, his breathing, even sensing him watching her—the entire time.

Was this her imagination again or something more?

She hoped the latter, because now that he'd found his smile and manners, her attraction to him kept growing.

It took less than a minute to put away the game.

She stood. Her muscles were tight after sitting on the floor for so long. "I need to move."

"Same."

As he rose and stretched, his movements—okay, *he*—captivated her. She swallowed.

"The room next door has a table." He motioned to the boxes on the dresser. "We could use that to do a puzzle next."

Anything would be better than her staring at him like a lovesick teenager. She blinked to stop focusing on him. "Sure."

He grabbed a puzzle and showed her the picture on the box. "Does a beach scene work for you?"

Lying on a white-sand beach on a tropical island with

him wouldn't suck. Not that she'd traveled anywhere like that except between the pages of books and on television.

Someday…

Though most likely not with Adam. She shook off the twinge of disappointment with a smile. "A blue, sunny sky sure beats the weather outside."

As if on cue, thunder rumbled.

Cambria ignored it the same way she'd pretended pounding rain hadn't been pelting the roof and windows for hours and another mudslide wasn't possible. Earlier, Adam had shown her how to apply online for a life insurance quote. If only she'd thought to do that before.

A familiar ache in her stomach reminded her that it must be close to dinnertime. She hadn't eaten today, so she was hungry. "I'll be right back."

In the bathroom, Cambria washed her hands. With only one set of reusable bamboo utensils, she would make Adam's meal first, and then she would eat after him.

In the bedroom, she fixed him a plate with a bit of everything. The water in the carafe was more warm than hot, but she filled the noodle cup with it and closed the foil lid. She tore off a paper towel to use as a napkin, tucked a water bottle under her arm, and carried his dinner into the other room.

Adam sat at the table and typed on his phone. The puzzle pieces were piled in front of him.

"Any news?" Cambria asked.

"Not yet."

She set the plate on the corner of the table and handed

him the water. "Dinner is served."

His forehead creased. "Where's your food?"

"I only have one set of utensils, so we'll eat in shifts." She motioned to the food. "Go on."

He hesitated.

"The sooner you eat, the sooner it'll be my turn."

As he ate, she turned the pieces right side up and separated the edges from the middle ones.

Her cell phone rang, and she removed it from her pocket. The call was from Lycaon. Matteo, the manager, must want to check in with her. That was nice of him.

"I need to take this," she said to Adam.

"Go ahead."

Smiling, she tapped the screen. "Hello."

"It's our busiest night, and you're not here. Do you think the dishes wash themselves? Where are you?" Matteo demanded.

Every muscle bunched. She gripped the phone. "There was a mudslide. I'm stuck in Hood Hamlet. I left a message with Adriana a few hours ago. She said she'd tell you I wouldn't be in tonight."

Several curses followed.

Cambria flinched.

"I spoke with Adriana before she left. She didn't mention you at all."

"She must have forgotten."

"You've lied for the last time!" He shouted so loudly the sound hurt Cambria's ear.

Her chest tightened. "I'm not lying. I'm trapped."

"And I'm sure your grandfather had a heart attack the last time you missed a shift."

Tears stung her eyes. "He did. I couldn't leave my grandmother alone during his surgery."

"You're fired."

"No." She struggled to breathe. Tears fell. "Please, don't fire me. I'm telling the truth."

"You'll be paid for the hours you worked this week, but you won't get a recommendation."

Her shoulders shook, but she held back a sob. "You don't understand. I need this job. I'll do—"

Adam took the phone from her hand and held it to his ear. "Who is this? ... Hello, Matteo, this is Adam Zeile. ... Yes, I enjoyed my dinner there last week, but I won't eat at Lycaon ever again, and I'll tell all my friends why. ... Well, I'm trapped with Cambria in Hood Hamlet because of a mudslide." His eyes were dark, and his jaw tense. "You should have believed her. ... Dishwashers should be treated with respect, too. ... I own a distillery in town, and she's better off working there than at Lycaon."

With that, he hit the end button, disconnecting the call.

Tears on her face, she stared in disbelief. No one besides her grandparents had ever stepped up for her as Adam had done. "I…"

He touched her arm with his free hand. "I'm sorry for taking over like that, but I hated to see you so upset and I had to do something. Forgive me?"

The way his gaze focused on her sent Cambria's pulse sprinting. "Of course, I'm so grateful you did that. I never expected Matteo to react that way. I did leave a message earlier."

"I believe you."

Three words that sent heat flowing through her. "Thank you."

Her phone rang again, startling Cambria.

As Adam glanced at the screen, his expression hardened more. He handed the cell phone to her. "It's the restaurant. I'm sure Matteo is calling to say he's not firing you. Based on what I've seen today, I have no doubt you're an excellent employee, but he also doesn't want to lose customers."

"I know." Cambria, however, needed to be realistic about her situation. "But I need the paycheck."

She went to accept the call, but Adam grabbed her hand. "Wait."

The phone rang again. "Why?"

"I meant what I said about you being better off working at my whiskey distillery." He let go of her hand and rubbed his forehead with his index finger. "I'm not involved in the daily operations, but we're hiring part-time and full-time employees. The managers will treat you fairly and be more understanding than Matteo."

Stuff like this didn't happen to her. The next ring made her want to mute her phone. "Full-time is an option?"

As he nodded, his gaze remained locked on her. He cleared his throat. "Just tell me you're interested, and I'll message the manager to let him know you can start this coming week."

Adam was a good luck charm. A smile spread across her face.

"Yes." Cambria ignored the call—something she never imagined herself doing. Excitement had her wiggling her toes. "You have no idea how interested I am. Full-time would be a dream come true, but part-time would be great. Either would be awesome."

"The choice is yours." Strange, but his tone sounded almost wistful.

"I-I…" The job offer was too good to be true. Doubts rose up. Cambria wanted to ignore them, but she didn't want to have regrets later. "This is so generous of you, but why are you offering me a job?"

"It's simple." Adam's lips parted, and his smile left her breathless. "You've been helping me. Now it's my turn to help you. Your neighbor told me you were good people, and he's correct. You are."

His words made her feel tingly all over and gave her chills at the same time. "Did Sam tell you anything else?"

Adam nodded. "He mentioned the eviction. He doesn't want you to live in your car. I don't want that, either."

The kindness in Adam's eyes, the concern in his voice, made her want to believe he cared. Because why else would he have offered her a job? But no matter how hard she tried, she couldn't ignore the truth.

And that hurt.

She turned away from him. "I-I don't have a choice."

More tears poured from her eyes. Happy ones. Sad ones. The emotions she'd held in for months burst out like a levee giving way. She'd tried to be strong for her grandparents, but keeping it under control was no longer possible.

"Hey." Adam wrapped his arms around her and pulled her against his chest. "Trust me. It'll all work out."

She appreciated him trying to comfort her, but there was no winning lottery ticket or happily ever after waiting for her. She'd done her best. Unfortunately, it hadn't been good enough. In a week, she would be homeless. It wasn't only the rent she couldn't afford. She was behind with all her bills. No job would change that.

Unable to stop the flow of tears, she cried harder.

"Let it out." Adam held on to her, rubbing circles on her back the way her grandma had when she was younger.

Cambria cried, clinging to him, not caring what she looked like or what he might think. For how long? She had no idea, but she would probably be embarrassed if she did. Still, Adam didn't let go of her. She relished being in his arms, inhaling his scent, and soaking up his strength—something she desperately needed.

"I don't know how I'll ever be able to thank you." The words came out disjointed in between sobs. Her breathing was ragged. "I really don't."

He brushed his lips over her hair. "You just did."

More tears fell. Adam was too sweet. A real-life guardian angel. "You must think I'm a total flake. Being evicted. Losing my job."

He hugged her tighter. "I don't think that. Something must have happened and things spiraled."

"Spiraled so bad." She forced the words from her thick throat. She should let go of him, but she didn't want to. He was all that was holding her up—literally and figuratively.

"You don't have to tell me."

Except she wanted to.

"When Beck and Hunter moved to Las Vegas, they left me with the lease for a three-bedroom apartment. They paid for one extra month of rent, but I couldn't find roommates." Cambria sniffled. "I needed time off when my grandfather had a heart attack, so they cut my shifts at the bakery and the restaurant. Each month, I've scraped together the payments for my grandparents' place, but there's not much left over. Okay, none. But as long as I'm able to pay for what they need, I can handle anything."

"You can." Adam loosened his hold on her and looked at her face. "But you shouldn't have to. I'll help you."

"You're giving me a job." As he stared into her eyes, something shifted in her chest. She didn't know what, but it was beautiful and overwhelming and downright terrifying. "That's enough."

"I want to do more." His voice was so soft, so caring. He wiped tears from her face. "Please let me help you and your grandparents."

Cambria wanted to throw herself against him again and let him help her. Who was she kidding? She wanted him to make everything better. She sniffled again.

"It's not your responsibility. My parents dumped Beck and me at a campground near Bend. My grandma and grandpa took us in. They'd been saving for retirement but ended up spending that money to raise us. Now they're left with what they get from Social Security each month, which isn't enough to pay for where they live. So I make up the difference." Cambria was rambling again, but she didn't care. "Sam offered to help me, but I've never asked for money. I want to be the person my grandparents were to me and my brother. They gave us so much. Now, it's my turn. I need to take care of them."

"Who takes care of you?"

She didn't want to answer, but he deserved one. "Me," she whispered.

"Oh, sweetheart." His tender tone washed over her like a caress. "That's so admirable, but even the most self-reliant people I know need a break now and then."

She wanted to believe him. "I don't want to feel less than enough. Or be a burden. That's what my parents called me and Beck."

"You aren't a burden. You're a blessing and a gift." Adam smoothed her hair. "Accepting help can be uncomfortable at first, but I promise you'll never be less."

Cambria remained unconvinced. He was just being kind because who would offer to help without knowing more of the situation or how much she contributed for her grandparents' place or how much she owed and needed to get back on track. "It's a lot of money."

"I can afford it." A smile tugged on his lips, one that made him look younger, more approachable, and even hotter than before. "Will you please let me help? If not for you, then for your grandparents."

Maybe he was her lucky charm. She'd been called practical by everyone she knew, but she was also smart enough to say yes. "For my grandparents."

He laughed.

She wished she could hear the deep, rich sound every single day of her life. "What's so funny?"

Adam tapped the tip of her nose. "I never thought I'd have to work that hard to give someone money."

It sounded as if there was a story there. She stared up at him. "Do you do this a lot?"

"Not like this." He cupped her face. "You're a special woman, Cambria Baker. I'm happy we're trapped together."

"Same." The word came out breathless, matching the way she felt.

A connection drew them closer, and Adam lowered his mouth to hers.

His kiss was gentle, almost tentative, but she soaked up his warmth and taste. As he pressed harder, she arched toward him, wanting more. Because somehow in this old cabin, trapped by a mudslide, Cambria discovered where she belonged.

She'd found home.

With him.

And she never wanted to leave.

Chapter Six

Adam had no clue why he was kissing Cambria. It might be her sweet smile or kind eyes or palpable affection for her grandparents. Whatever the reason, one kiss would never be enough. He had no idea how he knew, but his heart told him he'd found what Henry called the right woman.

There's someone for everyone.

Adam hadn't believed his friend, but Cambria was the one.

My one.

Still, rushing into anything when a few hours ago they feared for their lives wouldn't be smart. He would wait a few days—a week—before asking her to marry him. As strange as that might have seemed this morning when he woke up, it made perfect sense now.

Adam took a step back.

Her lips were swollen, and her chin was red from his beard.

Beautiful.

A smile lit up her face. "Wow."

"I was about to say that."

"But I have to ask. Was the kiss just a heat-of-the-moment thing?"

"No." The word catapulted out, but he wanted—needed—to explain better even if he wasn't sure himself. "It's hard for me to understand what's happening because we just met, but this is more than that. A lot more."

"We went through the mudslide together. Maybe the adrenaline rush and fear have heightened our senses and is making us want to feel more alive."

"Is that what you believe?"

"No." Her cheeks turned a charming shade of pink. "I mean, I hope it's not that. But I've never been through an experience like this or felt this way about someone so quickly or…"

He kissed her again. "Me, either. So let's just see what happens."

She gulped. "Tonight?"

"Tomorrow, and the day after, and the next one after that." If he mentioned more, she might freak out. "Sound good?"

Cambria nodded.

"You haven't eaten." He picked up his empty plate and the bamboo utensils. "Come on. We need to make you dinner."

She straightened. "We?"

"Yes, we." He kissed her forehead. "I'm not much of a cook, but I can manage this."

After she ate, they worked on the puzzle until they needed their cell phone flashlights to see. Then, they sat on the bed and talked about their families and their favorite things. They shared their first kisses, their biggest accomplishments, and their worst mistakes.

Adam mentioned his company and that he made enough he didn't worry about money. She'd quieted until admitting all she did was worry about money, so knowing he didn't do the same thing was a relief. He waited for the questions about his net worth, investment portfolio, and car. They never came. She only asked if he was happy.

Adam wanted to kick himself for lumping her in with all the gold diggers. The only thing gold about Cambria was her heart. And he promised himself she would never want for anything ever again. Nor would her grandparents, who had raised such a kindhearted woman.

Hours later, she fell asleep against him. His back and neck would hurt from sitting up all night, but he didn't care because holding her so close would be worth the pain.

As her chest rose and fell, Adam smoothed her hair. He'd never watched someone sleep, but now he didn't want to stop.

A text notification sounded.

He glanced at his phone.

Dash: *I have info on Cambria.*
Adam: *Thanks, but I don't need it.*
Dash: *Sure?*

Adam: *Positive. If there's an issue, we'll work it out.*
Dash: *You sound a lot like Wes.*
Adam: *Thanks for the compliment.*
Dash: *BTW, there's no red flags with Cambria.*
Adam: *Great. Now, get us out of here.*
Dash: *Just need better weather. Blaise has his helicopter and pilot ready. Kieran is coordinating with the local officials. Wes and Mason are helping with relief efforts for others affected by the mudslide. Brett's trying to stop Henry from giving away more of his money.*
Adam: *So just a typical day.*
Dash: *Yep.*

With one hand, he typed and sent another text.

Adam: *Is your guest house available?*
Henry: *Yes. Does someone need a place to stay?*
Adam: *The real estate agent.*
Henry: *It's Cambria's as long as she needs it.*
Adam: *Thanks, but how do you know her name?*
Henry: *I recently met her at an open house. Is she as sweet as she seems?*
Adam: *Sweeter.*
Henry: *I figured she was perfect for you.*
Adam: *Playing matchmaker again?*
Henry: *Did it work?*
Adam: *I'll let you know, but thanks.*
Henry: *That's what friends are for. Get some sleep. We'll have you out of there tomorrow.*

Typical Henry. Adam laughed until he glanced at Cambria against him. Though the guy might actually know what he was doing.

* * *

The next morning, Cambria woke up, cuddled against Adam. She hadn't slept so well in…forever, even though she wore everyday clothes, not pajamas, and was only partially covered with the wool blanket he'd found in the closet.

He smiled at her. "There's a break in the weather. A helicopter will pick us up soon."

Us. She liked the sound of that. Except… "What about my car?"

"That will have to wait a while, but I have one you can drive. My friend, Henry Davenport, has a guest house where you can stay, too."

The name sounded familiar. "Does Henry have a beautiful goddaughter named Noelle?"

Adam laughed. "Did he show you her photos?"

"Yes. Henry made a slow open house go by much faster, but his real estate agent wasn't amused."

"That's Henry for you." Adam straightened. "We should pack your stuff so we're ready when the helicopter arrives."

Her stomach churned. "I've never flown in one."

"It's not that different from a plane," he said matter-of-factly.

They came from such different worlds. He didn't think it was a problem, but still, she sighed. "I haven't flown in one of those, either."

"Then it's a day of firsts."

He hugged her, giving her the support she needed without her having to ask. This might work out.

"The helicopter belongs to my friend Blaise," Adam explained. "I'll be with you. There's nothing to worry about."

Less than an hour later, Cambria wore padded earphones and sat next to Adam in the helicopter. His fingers laced with hers, and she clung tightly to him.

As the helicopter lifted off the ground, he squeezed her hand. The cabin grew smaller until she could no longer see it.

Cambria hoped what they'd discovered while being trapped wouldn't fade away as quickly in the real world. But being on this helicopter, not knowing what would happen when they arrived at wherever they were headed, was nerve-wracking, but no matter what transpired, she was thankful for meeting Adam Zeile.

They landed at Timberline Lodge, where they were ushered to a triage center, questioned, examined, and let go. They walked outside where a group of men—handsome, though not as hot as Adam—stood. As soon as they saw him, they smiled and came forward.

Cambria stopped, fighting rising panic. Her car was still at the cabin. She had no idea how to get home or what would happen next.

"It's okay, sweetheart," Adam whispered. "My friends are here. And they'll love you as much as I do."

"You…" She couldn't bring herself to say the word.

"I do." He brushed his lips over hers. "As crazy as it might seem."

"Then I must be crazy, too."

And it was total insanity.

First, Adam introduced her to his friends. Henry greeted her with a hug and a kiss on the cheek as if they were long-lost friends, not people who'd met at an open house two weeks ago. Then, she met Blaise, Brett, Dash, Kieran, Mason, and Wes, who welcomed her to their friend group. She felt as if she'd gained seven more brothers in only a few minutes. Each of the men offered her help and jobs. She was touched and overwhelmed.

"Just get used to it," Adam whispered. "They like you, and friends help each other."

That evening, Cambria took him to meet her grandparents. She had a feeling her grandma and grandpa would love Adam as much as she did, and that turned out to be true. As she saw the three get along so well, her heart soared with happiness. After they said goodbye and headed to the car, Adam was on the phone to find a better facility for her grandparents. She didn't think she could love him more, but each day, her feelings for him grew.

He didn't seem to have that good of an impression of Beck, but the two spoke on the phone and got along, which was a relief.

One thing Cambria realized was Adam and his friends didn't waste time. Maybe it was their personalities, but each day passed by in a blur. She moved out of the apartment and into Henry's luxurious guest cottage. She completed her orientation days at Adam's distillery and worked with Brett Matthews on her finances.

She also realized real estate wasn't for her. She'd gotten her license to work with her brother, and no longer wanted to pursue that career path. With a full-time position at the distillery, she also quit her job at the bakery—no more being at work before sunrise. She also helped her grandparents get settled into the top-rated assisted living center in Portland. She had no idea how Adam managed that, but she was grateful. He was the one constant to her days, and she enjoyed seeing him, even if it was for a brief time.

On Saturday, one of Adam's security team drove them up to Timberline Lodge. She hadn't expected bodyguards—including one of her own—to come with her new boyfriend, but she'd discovered he was loaded. That freaked her out, but he was still her Adam, so she tried not to think about his money.

They enjoyed a lovely lunch in the dining room. Afterward, they headed outside. A few people skied on the glacier above them. The sky was a perfect cornflower blue with only wisps of white clouds floating by. The temperature was pleasant.

A perfect day.

She inhaled the fresh mountain air. "I can't believe how much has changed in only a week."

He held her hand. "Good changes, I hope."

"The best." Contentment flowed through her. "I love working at the distillery. My grandparents love their new place. And I love you."

"A trifecta." He raised her hand and kissed it. "I love

you, and it feels like I won, too."

"You still haven't found your dream property with the perfect view."

"I have you." Affection filled his eyes. "That's better than anything I could buy."

Her smile seemed to spread to the tips of her fingers and toes. "Good answer."

Two birds flew by.

"Thanks." He let go of her hand. "Now, it's your turn."

"For what?"

"To answer my question." Adam dropped on one knee and pulled a small box from his back pocket. "It's been a wild week, but each day, my feelings for you grow deeper and more intense. It's been ridiculously fast, but you are the one for me. I asked your grandparents for permission, and they agreed, so… Cambria Baker, will you do me the honor of marrying me and becoming my wife?"

Her mouth gaped, and she struggled to breathe. Tears blurred her vision.

"I-I… Yes! I'll marry you."

Adam stood and placed the ring on her finger. A perfect fit from the perfect-for-her guy.

Joy overflowed from her heart. He might have billions, but that didn't matter to her. Only he did. The other stuff was just icing as her grandma enjoyed saying. And this man was better than Cambria's favorite buttercream frosting. "I love you."

"I love you." He kissed her, a kiss full of love and forever.

Cambria couldn't wait to see what happened next.

Epilogue

Three weeks later…

Surrounded by his closest friends, Kieran O'Neal stood in the Silcox Hut at Mount Hood's Timberline Lodge. "Hut" seemed a misnomer given the stone walls and floors, wide windows, fireplace, and a timber-covered arched ceiling strung with lights. He hadn't known what to expect when Adam told him he was getting married in two weeks, but this was the perfect setting for the intimate wedding of a couple who'd met a few miles from here. What good was having billions, if the money didn't make special events happen as if by magic?

Henry Davenport bounced from foot to foot, as giddy as a kid in a toy store. "That's one tech geek down. Five more to go."

"Not me," Kieran and his four friends said in unison. "I don't have any interest in getting married."

"Me, either," Mason Reese agreed. "Why settle down when there are so many women out there?"

"That's what they all say until you meet the one." Brett Matthews took a sip from his drink.

"Or until I introduce you to her." Henry beamed as if he'd discovered a tree that grew branches full of money instead of leaves.

"Please." Brett rolled his eyes. "I gave you full credit for bringing Laurel and me together. But Adam and Cambria—"

"I arranged the showing at the cabin," Henry announced for the hundredth time that day. "If not for me, none of us would be here tonight. And Adam and Cambria wouldn't live happily ever after."

Mason smirked. "Keep believing that fairy tale, Henry. But we know the true story."

Dash Cabot nodded. "Adam thought Cambria was a gold digger. That's why he asked me to check her out while they were trapped together, but then he didn't want to know what I discovered. Not that there was anything bad."

"What have I told you about hacking, Wonderkid?" Wes Lockhart sounded more like a dad than the oldest of the group. "If you're arrested, your board will lose it."

"Who said anything about hacking?" Dash feigned innocence. "I was just helping a friend."

Wes shook his head. His hair was still short—he'd lost it all during his chemo treatments—but he looked healthier than he had in years. Now, all he had to do was stay in remission.

Kieran would drink to that, and did.

"You did your part, Master Dashiell." Henry bowed to

the Wonderkid. "But—"

"Mother Nature deserves credit because of the mudslide." Kieran loved Henry, but the guy needed to stop thinking he was the ultimate matchmaker. "Not even you could manage that."

"True." Henry tilted his head. "But I'll gladly take the assist."

"Good, now quit while you're ahead," Blaise Mortenson said.

Brett raised his glass. "Hear, hear. You've done enough, Henry."

"You'll see," Henry mumbled. "I'm just getting started."

Adam in a tuxedo and Cambria in a stunning white gown moved toward them, their feet barely touching the floor. They held hands. Their faces radiated such joy and love, it was almost palpable.

Kieran inhaled sharply. He had everything he ever wanted, but at this moment, he envied his friend for what he'd found—to have a woman gaze so lovingly into his eyes as if he'd handed over the stars, moon, and heavens.

From strangers to one true love in a week?

He'd had his doubts, but seeing these two today made Kieran want to believe it was possible.

"We'll be doing the bridal bouquet and garter toss soon." Adam raised Cambria's hand to his mouth and kissed it. "I expect to see all of you except Brett out there."

"Please." Cambria bounced as if she were rising on her tiptoes. "It's my grandma's favorite wedding tradition, so the more bachelors out there, the happier she'll be."

"Don't worry," Brett said confidently. "They'll be out there."

I'll make sure of it was implied.

"Thank you." Cambria was the definition of sweet, but she didn't hesitate going head-to-head with Adam, which he needed. He adored his bride and her family.

Adam stole a kiss from her. "I love you."

She sighed. "I love you so much."

If Adam weren't one of his best friends, the sugary sweetness between these two would make Kieran sick.

"Not worth half a billion dollars, huh?" Henry joked.

"You win," Adam conceded. "I'm an idiot."

Henry smirked. "Thank you. I expect to be named the godfather of your children."

Adam rolled his eyes, but Kieran noticed he hadn't said no.

"The wedding coordinator is ready for us, my love," Cambria said.

"See you gents later." Adam hurried away with his bride while all single ladies were invited to join in the bouquet toss.

A few minutes later, Cambria's brother's girlfriend clutched the bouquet with a silly grin on her face and diamond engagement rings flashing in her eyes.

"And now, will all the single gentlemen please come forward," a woman announced.

Kieran didn't hesitate. Adam would likely aim for his new brother-in-law, Beck, especially after the guy's girlfriend had caught the bouquet. How perfect would that be?

Dash and Mason joined him. Finally, Blaise, Wes, and Henry stepped up.

"This is just a myth, right?" Dash asked. "The person who catches it doesn't always get married next."

"It was an urban legend before those existed," Wes said in a matter-of-fact tone. "So if one of you finds yourself with the garter, don't drop it or you'll upset Adam, Cambria, and Mrs. Baker. Agreed?"

Everyone nodded.

Henry raised his two hands. Both held champagne flutes. "Or, you could be like me and not have a free hand to catch the garter."

"That's one way of stacking the cards in your favor," Blaise said.

"Okay, get ready," Mason warned.

The wisp of lace and blue fabric shot through the air. Unlike the women, who'd jumped for the flowers, none of them moved, including Beck. The garter flew directly at…

It hit Kieran's hands.

In shock, he nearly dropped the thing until he saw Adam and Cambria with light-up-the-room smiles.

He glanced at his relieved friends. Guess they hadn't wanted to catch it. He wasn't worried. "No big deal. Catching the garter means nothing."

"You have never been so wrong in your life." Henry surveyed the other guests. "The woman of your dreams might be here. But if she's not, no worries. I'll help you find her."

"No, thanks." As he laughed at Henry's pouty face, Kieran put the garter over his hand and jacket until it was around his bicep. "It's just a silly wedding custom."

But maybe tonight when Kieran closed his eyes and fell asleep, he would meet the woman in his dreams. He straightened the garter. Because she couldn't really exist, could she?

The Kiss Catcher

MELISSA McCLONE

Chapter One

July

W*here is he?*

Kieran O'Neal and his friend Henry Davenport stood in the CEO's office at Talk-View-Text, aka TVT. They planned to have lunch with Mason Reese. Only, Mason wasn't there. Not all that surprising, but Kieran had hoped the guy would show up on time.

For once.

"Relax." Henry studied a 3D wooden brain teaser puzzle sitting on a bookcase shelf. "I can hear the gears turning in your brain from here."

"I'm thinking."

"Which should be illegal on your lunch break. Emphasis on break. You don't need to be *on* and working all the time."

Except Kieran rarely turned himself off. If he did, he might lose...everything.

The software industry was fickle, and today's darling might end up in tomorrow's trash. He wouldn't let that happen. Not to himself, his family, nor his employees.

"You should thank Mason for leaving us to play in his office." Henry took the puzzle apart. "And the best part is you're with me. I'm the definition of fun."

"Depends on who's defining the word," Kieran joked.

See?

He wasn't a stick in the mud or always working. And Henry was correct about Mason's office with its large screen TVs, a conference area wired for the newest technologies, and the market's best gaming platforms. It was more playground than workplace. "But time is money."

"You have enough money to burn a bonfire-sized amount and not miss a penny."

True. Not that Kieran would.

His stomach churned, though that might be hunger. He'd skipped breakfast because of a busy morning. A video call had followed a meeting. There'd also been an interview with the business news channel. "I'm not used to this."

Henry raised a brow. "Doing nothing?"

Kieran shoved his fingertips into his pants pockets to keep from checking his inbox. The struggle was real. "Yeah."

"Adam saw the light, but the rest of you?" Henry rolled his eyes. He'd perfected the gesture to be over-the-top and in-your-face. Similar to his larger-than-life persona. "Work won't be the little spoon to your big spoon at night. It won't kiss you goodbye each morning in anticipation of seeing you again in a few hours."

Given his busy life, Kieran couldn't imagine either of those things happening. He would settle for someone to share a meal with occasionally. At least that was all he'd wanted until Saturday night.

Something had changed at Cambria and Adam's wedding.

Kieran kept trying to picture his perfect woman. The qualities kept changing, probably because he questioned her existence.

His friends—well, some of them—wholeheartedly believed she did.

Adam, Brett, and Henry claimed there was someone— the love of a lifetime—for each person. But Kieran doubted that. He was thirty-two. If she were real, wouldn't he have met her by now?

He wouldn't mention that to Henry. Otherwise, the guy would never leave him alone.

"Blaise is more of a workaholic than me." Kieran respected his friend's drive. He never let up trying to make his financial company the best it could be. "Wes used to be the worst of us all."

Until cancer made Wes re-prioritize his life. Even in remission now, he limited his work hours and spent long weekends at his lodge in Hood Hamlet, which was where Kieran had stayed the night of Adam and Cambria's wedding at Timberline Lodge's Silcox Hut on Mount Hood.

He didn't understand the changes Wes had made to his life. But Kieran had never experienced a serious illness. It had been hard enough watching Wes go through his treatment and support the man who was a big brother to all of them.

"Stop comparing yourself to others." Henry returned the puzzle—now in pieces—to its place before moving closer to Kieran. "You caught the garter. Unless you slow down and pay attention to more than work, your perfect woman will show up, but you'll be too busy to notice, and she'll end up married to someone else."

If she were even real… "You guys aren't going to let me forget I caught that thing."

"Nope." Henry sounded pleased. "You shouldn't expect us to. I have no stake in the last-single-man-standing bet, but Blaise, Dash, Mason, and Wes want to win. At the reception, Blaise said the pot should reach half a billion by September."

Five years ago, Mason had proposed a bet. The entry fee was ten million dollars. Brett Matthews hadn't been part of their group yet, and Henry had declined to enter. That had left the six of them, known as the Billionaires of Silicon Forest, to take the wager. Blaise Mortenson's company used a beta investing algorithm to manage the sixty million dollars. The results exceeded everyone's expectations and increased their desire to be the last single man standing.

"With that much money as an incentive to stay single, why date?" Kieran asked.

Henry shuddered. "Because not dating would…suck."

"I suppose it would."

Ever since seeing Adam and Cambria so in love, Kieran envied their closeness. Something he'd never felt. At least not anything more profound than surface-level affection. He dated, but his net worth was the draw to women, not him.

Or his heart.

"I wouldn't mind meeting someone," Kieran admitted. "Though, I might have better luck blowing kisses and seeing who catches one than trying to find a woman who wants to date me, not my money."

"Try tossing diamonds. You'll have a better success rate than with kisses."

"Ha-ha." He forced himself not to roll his eyes as Henry did. Then Kieran remembered something. "Hey, didn't you do something similar?"

"A folly of youth." Henry brushed it aside. "But dating isn't a chore."

"Not for a guy like you who eschews serious relationships and has casual dating down to an art form."

"It wouldn't be fair to the women of the world if only one of them got me." Henry spoke in a serious tone as if he were discussing world peace. He poked at Kieran's chest. "But you need to relax. That's R-E-L-A-X. A word not in your vocabulary. Once you unwind and chill, it'll happen."

"What will?"

"Love." Henry's lips curved upward in a goofy grin. "True love, hearts, red roses, violins, and marriage vows. Just ask Adam."

Kieran snickered. "I would, except he's on his honeymoon and threatened bodily harm to anyone who disturbs him and Cambria until they return."

"I rest my case." A smug expression settled on Henry's face.

The way he waxed on about other people's romances amused Kieran. Despite Henry's denials of never settling down, the guy would fall hard and fast for someone the same way Adam had. Kieran couldn't wait to see that happen. "It'll take more than relaxing to find…"

Kieran didn't want to name what he wanted. He wasn't one hundred percent sure what it was or if it were possible.

"In that case…" Henry rubbed his chin. "There's a woman named Hadley. She's a skilled matchmaker in San—"

"No." Kieran held up both hands to emphasize the point. He needed to stop whatever Henry had in mind. The guy cycled between a dog with a bone and a runaway train. In this case, he would be the latter. Better not let any momentum build, or Henry would demolish everything in his path. "I'm not getting caught up in your matchmaking games."

Henry's chest puffed out. "Oh, I like the sound of games. That's much better than Brett's 'schemes.'"

During one of Henry's outrageous birthday adventures—a tacky wedding in Reno—he'd set up Brett and Laurel Matthews. The resulting marriage was supposed to last only one night. "Semantics."

Henry harrumphed. "Wait and see."

"I *am* waiting." Kieran glanced at the time. "Should we go without Mason?"

"Please look up the definition of relaxing in whatever online dictionary you use because you're doing it wrong or ignoring me. I can't believe it's the latter." Henry shook his head. "And what's the problem with waiting? I have no pressing engagements."

The billionaire trust-fund baby wouldn't. He'd never worked a day in his life. Between Brett and Blaise, whose companies managed billions of Henry's inheritance, his money kept growing to ridiculous levels. A good thing because Henry's generous heart meant he gave away enormous amounts. He was known for his philanthropy and extravagant birthday parties.

"Some of us must work." Kieran typed a text to his assistant to reschedule his one o'clock. He'd given a heads-up to the division head he was meeting with, but updating him was the responsible thing to do. "Mason is becoming as bad as Dash."

"No one is as bad as Wonderkid, but I'll give Mason second place."

"Second place for what?" Mason entered his office. He wore gray pants and a button-up shirt. No tie was typical for the coder turned billionaire whose social media app put others to shame, but he likely kept a suit jacket and tie somewhere in the office for meetings and interviews.

"For being inconsiderate of other people's time." Kieran glanced at his phone. "You did something similar after the wedding when you never showed up at the bar."

Mason rolled his eyes. "First, Dash is more inconsiderate than me, but that's his nature, ingrained in his DNA, and not personal. And I'm not in second place. That spot belongs to Henry, who only wears an expensive watch as a fashion accessory or to show off. He never looks at the time."

Henry beamed. "That is true."

"Me?" Mason pointed to himself. "I needed to discuss

an issue with our development team. It was either be inconsiderate to them and, by default, our stockholders if I arrived on time for our lunch or meet with them and be a few minutes late with you two. Easy decision, and one I would make again."

"Not a few. Twenty," Kieran corrected. "Though we would have made the same choice."

Henry gasped.

"Don't lump me in with all of you who *work*." He spoke the last word as if it were offensive. To him, it probably was. "I would have blown off both parties, so I didn't offend one over the other, and found a pretty employee to take to lunch instead."

Kieran laughed to himself. He had no desire to encourage Henry, but what the guy said was typical.

"It's a good thing I'm not you." Mason placed his tablet on his desk. "Let's go. Anybody up for Taco Tuesday?"

"Mason?" a feminine voice asked.

Henry wagged his eyebrows. "Or let's not go and stay here."

"Stop," Mason whispered. "Come in, Selah."

Mason had mentioned Selah a few times. The woman had sounded competent, if not a hardnose, but Mason needed someone capable of standing up to him. She must be older with sons because she had the skills to handle her boss.

A young, attractive woman with copper hair wasn't who Kieran expected to see.

Three steps into the office, she froze. "I'm sorry, Mase. I didn't realize you were busy."

"No worries. I was just about to go out to lunch with friends." Mason motioned her forward, and she went, albeit reluctantly. "Selah, meet Kieran O'Neal and Henry Davenport. Guys, this is the person who keeps things headed in the right direction, Selah Burton."

"That's right." Amusement gleamed in her green eyes. She waved a manila folder in the air. "I steer the HMS TVT. If my boss had control of the rudder, we'd have run aground at least a dozen times by now."

Henry tapped his chin. "Who works for whom here?"

Selah's grin lit up her face. "Mason is the boss, but the last thing he needs is another person saying yes to whatever he says. That's why he keeps me around."

Kieran's heart sped up as if he'd scored tickets on the SpaceX Crew Dragon capsule. She captivated him.

Mason nodded. "Truth."

"Nice to meet you, Selah." Kieran extended his arm. As soon as he touched her hand, his brain short-circuited. Her skin was so soft.

"Are you Kieran or Henry?" she asked, letting go of his hand.

"Kieran." His mouth was Sahara dry. He swallowed again. "Kieran O'Neal."

"I'm Henry. And I have a brilliant idea." Henry strode forward like a heat-seeking missile locked on a target. "Would you like to join us for lunch, Selah?"

Kieran would like to get to know her better. "You're more than welcome."

"Thank you." Selah didn't hesitate to answer. "But I can't."

Can't because she has another lunch date?

It was none of Kieran's business, but he wanted to hear the answer.

She handed the folder to Mason. "You forgot this at the meeting."

Mason took it. "Thanks. The changes—"

"I made them. Enjoy your lunch." Selah smiled at each of them. "Watch out for this guy. He'll eat in ten minutes unless he has a meeting scheduled. If that's the case, he'll do anything to get out of it."

Mason laughed. "You're giving away my secrets."

She shrugged, not appearing the least bit repentant. "You said they're your friends. They must know you better than I do."

"Most of what we know isn't polite to say in mixed company." Henry flashed a charming smile, though Kieran thought the guy was trying way too hard.

"It sounds like we know similar things." Her tone was playful and mysterious.

She intrigued him.

"Nice meeting you. See you later," Selah said to Mason before leaving the office.

Kieran stared at the last spot where she'd stood. "Is she married?"

"Selah?" Mason asked.

Was there another woman in there? Kieran blew out a breath. "Yes, Selah."

"No, she's dated no one since she kicked her ex-boyfriend to the curb six months ago. A good thing because she deserves so much better than that loser." Mason studied him. "Why?"

"Because she's gorgeous." Henry sounded giddy. "And our Kieran appears smitten with Selah."

"Smitten?" Kieran asked.

Henry shrugged. "Alliteration. Go with it."

"She's attractive, and I would like to invite her to have coffee or dinner. Can I get her number?"

"No, no, no." Henry rubbed his palms together. "Coffee and dinner are so…"

"Normal," Mason offered.

Henry nodded. "Too normal. A woman who is both intelligent and beautiful needs more."

"That may be true," Mason agreed. "Selah has been down on men for months. I suggest you get to know her more subtlety. I'm happy to give you tips."

Kieran stared in disbelief. "You're the least subtle person—"

Henry cleared his throat.

"Excuse me." Kieran would admit he was wrong. "After Henry, you're the least subtle person in Portland if not the world. So I'm not sure what you're suggesting."

"Leave it to us," Henry said.

"Excuse me?" Kieran asked.

"Mason and I will figure out the best way for you to get together with Selah," Henry said.

That didn't sound like a good idea. Everything inside of Kieran told him to say no. But these were his friends. "Uh, asking her out is the simplest."

Mason shook his head. "If you do that, she might just say no."

Henry agreed as if he'd suddenly become an expert on the woman he'd just met. "Don't worry. We've got you."

Mason beamed. "Leave it to us."

The instinct that had made Kieran a billionaire protested. "I can handle this on my own. Coffee or dinner are safe bets. That's worked in the past."

Henry shook his head. "Not really, or you wouldn't be single and need a date."

"I don't need a date." Kieran needed nothing, but he wanted to get to know Selah. That meant not blowing his shot with her, if Mason was correct.

Henry clucked his tongue. "Going out for coffee or dinner is a date."

True, but the "date" carried more weight than the other words.

Kieran debated whether to trust his friends. His gaze bounced between the two men. "What did you have in mind?"

"We need to make a plan first," Henry said before Mason could answer.

The muscles in Kieran's shoulders relaxed. A plan meant they would put thought into this. "Please keep me informed."

He didn't want to be caught off guard by them.

Or with Selah.

Chapter Two

Early Wednesday morning in her office, Selah sipped a mocha. She preferred stronger coffee drinks, but she'd slept enough last night, and this flavor had sounded delicious when the barista suggested it. A half-eaten bagel lay on a napkin on her desk. Breakfast, however, could wait.

She focused on one of her four monitors, checking the project milestones on the update to the product that had made TVT a household name and her beyond-her-wildest-dreams wealthy. She wasn't a billionaire like Mason, but her company stock was worth more money than she could spend in a hundred lifetimes. Sure, she could retire now, but that lifestyle would…bore her.

There was more to life than work, but Selah enjoyed what she did and didn't want to do anything else right now. Besides, her boss needed her. She was the first employee Mason had hired for his start-up. He'd only been twenty-one and looked younger than that. Despite his in-need-of-a-cut hair, pale skin from being inside too much, sweatpants full of holes, and stained hoodies, his brilliant mind had shone through. She'd been a teaching assistant, but even as a lowly TA, she'd recognized something unique that set him apart from other students when they'd met his sophomore year. When he asked her to join his company, she'd jumped at the opportunity.

A wise decision for her career and net worth, two things she hadn't considered years ago. Mason's excitement and passion had been contagious. Though, she'd upset her parents and professors by dropping out of grad school to follow some "geek kid."

Selah had zero regrets.

Nearly a decade later, Mason was a boss and the closest thing to an annoying younger brother she had. She watched out for him.

Somebody had to do it.

Red text on the project software caught her attention.

Ugh. Selah's shoulders sagged.

Quality assurance had missed a milestone—a big one—even after the director told her they would complete their checks by five o'clock yesterday. Mason usually worked late, so when he'd asked to leave early, she gladly offered to cover for him and spent the afternoon attending a meeting in his place.

Now she would have to be hard-nosed about the delay. Issues added up fast, and the upgrade needed to be released on time.

Or early, if she had her say.

She pulled up her email. Mason wouldn't be happy about the missed milestone, but he would downplay the effects.

That was why she was the Shibu Inu to his golden retriever. He was a visionary who got lost in the big picture. His realm was the forest. The individual trees never registered, even when one had the power to topple everything. He ignored the nitty-gritty details and steps. Not on purpose, but because those things never entered his mind.

The idea and the final product held meaning for him. He'd been the same during group projects in college. Only now, the stakes were higher, with over fifteen thousand employees working at TVT and amounts of money with way too many zeroes hanging in the balance. More than once, someone suggested Mason should be on the board and hire another CEO to run the company, but he hadn't wanted to do that. She understood, which meant it was up to her to make all those bits and pieces work so the end product matched his vision.

Selah's fingers flew on her keyboard. The clicking of keys soothed her like hearing a favorite song on the car radio and lessened her frustration.

Don't mess with mama bear.

This company was as much her baby as it was Mason's.

If TVT wanted to remain the industry leader, they needed a flawless launch. When the new version went live, any errors or system issues would have their competitors jumping for joy and taking advantage of the mistakes. But if the updated version worked as Mason visualized—and she'd calculated—TVT would continue to be the standard upon which people judged the other social media platforms.

She hit send.

The email would make the director squirm, which was the point.

Selah added a note to the flowchart. The way it automatically formatted brought a groan. Newer software would suit their needs—okay, hers—better. But Mason wouldn't consider buying anything but DigiSoftKO, which was his friend Kieran's company. Her boss was loyal to his friends and employees, so she didn't fault him. The program had a few pluses in its favor, but they would use something else if it were up to her.

Someone knocked on her door, which was ajar. Mason stuck his head in her office. "Got a minute?"

He wasn't a micromanager, which meant there was only one reason for his visit.

"What do you need?" she asked.

Mason entered and plopped into the chair on the other side of her desk. "A favor."

That was nothing new. Part of Selah's job was to keep things running smoothly, including his life. To do that, she doled out favors like watermelon slices on the Fourth of July.

Selah expected Mason to pick up the Rubik's Cube she kept for him, since he enjoyed keeping his hands busy. Except he didn't touch it. That was odd.

"A work-related favor?" she asked.

Mason rubbed his neck. "Sort of. It's also personal."

That was unusual. She leaned forward. "What's going on?"

"My friend Kieran. He was here with Henry yesterday."

An image of Kieran's hazel eyes and gorgeous face

formed in her mind. Her temperature shot up.

Wait. Not gorgeous. Attractive. Yes, that was what he was. Selah swallowed.

No more admiring pretty boys. Forget about crushing on one, even from afar. They only broke a woman's heart. "I remember him."

"His company is starting an important project, and he needs it to go smoothly." Mason leaned forward, resting his elbows on his thighs. "He thought bringing in someone from the outside might be best. You're so good with kickoffs I thought you could help him."

She blinked, trying to comprehend what her boss wanted. This wasn't part of her responsibilities, so she got where the favor came in. Even so, he couldn't be serious. "Wait a minute. You want me to take time off in the middle of our biggest project since TVT's debut to help your friend? Or does that mean I'll be working there and here?"

A sheepish expression crossed Mason's face. "It shouldn't take long. You can organize something like this in your sleep, and you're familiar with the software they use. What if you spent mornings there and afternoons here?"

That might work, but Selah hesitated. She only trusted herself to keep their project on track. Control issues, yes, but they came in handy at TVT. "Things could fall apart here."

Mason's lips curved upward. The guy's features had matured, but at times like now, he still reminded her of that eager teenager she'd met during his sophomore year of college. "If anyone can pull it off, it's you."

"True, but I don't delegate well." Trust was an issue for

her. She could forgive, but forgetting wasn't easy. Logically, a couple of hours away from work wasn't that big of a deal, except they were coming to the crux of the project, where delays would affect the launch. "My assistant can deal with any calls, but if something needs to be handled while I'm away—"

"I'll take care of it."

Selah rolled her eyes. "Mase, this isn't something to hand off to your assistant. You might have to get on people if they make mistakes or mess up."

"I can't be mean like you." He stiffened. "Not that you're mean. But you can be intimidating."

"Only when people screw up." Mason didn't pay her to sit around and play nice. "If I'm not here, you can't visit the lab to discuss processing times. Got it?"

Mason sighed. "Yes. You should be able to get things squared away with Kieran quickly."

"So there's not much to do?"

He stared at his hands. "I'm not sure exactly."

"What do you know?"

His gaze met hers. "That one of my best friends needs you."

He was loyal like that. When potential investors wanted her replaced during the early round of funding, he'd walked away from their offer. "You've always spoken highly of Kieran."

"He has thousands of employees working for him, but no one's as good as you."

Pride filled her. She sat taller. "True again."

"So you'll do it?"

Selah nodded. "When do you want me to start?"

"This morning."

She startled. "Huh?"

A satisfied expression spread across Mason's face. "After you finish your breakfast and whatever you're doing right now, of course."

"Of course." The guy operated in another realm.

"If anything comes up, I'll be in touch."

That told her she would end up at the office this weekend, catching up on stuff. Not unusual for her, but… "Do you know anything about Kieran's project?"

Mason's gaze zeroed in on the Rubik's Cube. "No actual details."

"I hope this means they're finally updating their software."

"You mentioned a delay. One nanosecond versus two."

"It was—"

"Nothing a normal user would notice."

"So I'm what? Abnormal?"

"No, you're organized, focused, and want everything to be the way you like it. Kieran's product is rated number two in the market. A slight delay doesn't matter to anyone who isn't you."

So what if Selah had high standards with the applications she used? The software could be number one with a few improvements. "There are other issues besides the lag."

"Tell Kieran."

She tilted her head, remembering the list she'd put

together for Mason. He'd told her she worked for TVT, not DigiSoftKO. But she was sort of working for the other company now. She would take a printout of the document with her. "I will."

As he nodded, mischief gleamed in his eyes. "Your sense of responsibility demands you mention it, but no ice pick in the forehead bluntness, please."

Her shoulders squared. "I only say what's required."

"Which is a strength, Selah. And what makes you so valuable to me and TVT. Kieran shares your work ethic, but he's…sensitive. Remember that adage about honey instead of vinegar?"

"No one has ever called me sweet." Not even her parents, who were professors, intellectuals who lavished her with books, computers, and lab kits while she was growing up. They'd considered toys and dolls frivolous, a waste of her brilliant mind. But now, she had a guest bedroom that contained a doll collection and a bed covered with large stuffed animals. Both would mortify her mom and dad, but they were too busy doing their research projects in their respective ivory towers to visit her. Phone calls had dwindled to seasonal or national holidays.

Mason's gaze narrowed. "What about Axel?"

Heat rushed up Selah's neck to her face. Axel Oliver had seemed like a dream come true. They'd met at TVT when he worked as a contract employee. She'd broken her rule about dating a colleague because he'd been so perfect and promised to keep their relationship quiet at the office.

Axel had been Selah's opposite—a man who made her

relax and have fun. He was also hot. She'd fallen hard and fast, believing in her heart of hearts Axel was the one. He was charming and had quickly wrapped her around his little finger. She hadn't cared one bit.

When he proposed, she'd said yes, thinking all her dreams were coming true—until he'd wanted to fly and elope in Las Vegas that night. Warning bells had sounded in her head, cautioning her to slow down. She'd asked him to sign a prenup first—something Mason and her attorney had told her to do if she ever fell in love. Axel, however, had said no, throwing a literal tantrum, calling her an ice queen and unlovable, and telling her he was better off with his real fiancée. The guy had been cheating on Selah the entire time and only wanted her money.

"No." That was all she wanted to say about him.

She never called Axel her ex-boyfriend because that made her feel stupid for being taken in by his pretty-boy looks—her type, unfortunately—and fake charm. She tried not to put what Axel did on other men, but Mason was one of the few she trusted these days.

He brushed his hands through his hair. "Pretend you're talking to a kid or a kitten or a puppy. Something cute and cuddly that makes you go mushy inside."

None of those things described Kieran O'Neal, but she enjoyed volunteering at a local Humane Society. A kitten's purr melted her heart. She would imagine one when she spoke with him. "I'll dial myself down a few notches."

Mason gave her a thumbs up. "Text me what I need to be aware of while you're gone this morning."

"I'll send an email, so check your inbox, please." As she thought about the number of his unread emails, Selah shivered. This time away had disaster written all over it. Her shoulder muscles bunched. "If Kieran's project can wait—"

"It can't. I'm up for this." Mason sounded confident, but he always did. "What's the worst thing that could happen?"

The urge to remind him of when she had the flu last winter sat on the tip of her tongue. Thankfully, the stock rebounded quickly.

"Remember, if this goes sideways." And something inside her screamed it would. "It was your idea."

Chapter Three

At his desk, Kieran studied the code on his monitor. His once steaming coffee must be lukewarm. He'd taken only one sip, but he didn't mind. He would rather troubleshoot the issue—something he did little of these days. Diving into the software's technical parts took time he rarely had, but he enjoyed solving problems.

His cell phone buzzed.

A glance at the screen showed a text notification from Mason. It wasn't from their group chat, which was unusual.

Kieran picked up his phone and read.

Mason: *Heads up! Selah is on her way to your office.*

Kieran did a double-take. He reread the text before typing furiously.

Kieran: *Why?*
Mason: *Henry and I said we'd help you.*
Kieran: *Why is she coming here this morning?*

It made no sense.

Dots appeared on his screen, but no message popped up.

Kieran grimaced. "Come on, Mase."

His assistant buzzed him. "Selah Burton is here to see you. She said you were expecting her."

He gritted his teeth. Mason and Henry needed to pay for whatever they'd done. Kieran got the feeling it wouldn't be good. He smoothed his hair and straightened his tie.

Please let this go well. "Send her in."

Another text notification sounded as the door opened, but he didn't have time to read it.

Kieran stood.

His chair rolled backward until it crashed against the wall.

Heat flooded his face—something that rarely happened. Selah's visit surprised him. Nothing else. "Hey."

Selah entered the office wearing a pair of navy pants and a short-sleeved button-up blouse. A black laptop bag hung off her shoulder. Mason had mentioned she'd worked with him to improve his image. Now Kieran saw why. She dressed stylishly, yet comfortably.

Rays of sunlight through the windows made her hair shine. His stomach filled with flutters.

Or nerves.

Most likely nerves over not knowing why she was here.

She smiled and his pulse sped up. "Good morning."

For now, at least.

Kieran swallowed the lump in his throat. He motioned

to an empty chair on the other side of his desk. "Have a seat."

She removed the strap and sat. "Mason told me you need help with a project?"

"Project?" Kieran hoped he didn't sound as dazed and confused as he felt. But he had no idea what she meant.

Selah nodded. Her dangling earrings chimed. "TVT is in the middle of a major update, so the timing isn't the best, but Mason said this was important. He also mentioned it wouldn't take long. I can spend mornings here with whoever is leading the project. Perhaps a Saturday or two."

"Me," he blurted.

"Excuse me?"

Breathe, O'Neal. "I'm in charge of the project."

The mythical one. Kieran balled his hands. Henry and Mason were going to pay.

"Or will be." Kieran cleared his dry throat before flexing his fingers. "When it launches."

All he needed to do was come up with a project. But he hated being dishonest.

Not his fault.

He blamed his so-called best friends. That didn't stop his shirt collar from tightening. Kieran forced himself not to tug on his tie.

Her gaze narrowed. "I had no idea you took such a hands-on approach."

Kieran shrugged. That was better than cringing. He motioned to his computer. "I'm reviewing code right now."

Not a lie.

He'd been doing that before she arrived, even if it wasn't

part of his daily responsibilities.

She half laughed. "Mason loves coding more than he enjoys running his company."

"I understand that. Coding is more fun than mingling with people who want to sell you something or buy your product at a big discount. But starting DigiSoftKO was my dream, so I can't complain."

When he'd been in his early twenties, Kieran hadn't realized what being so successful would mean. He'd never run DigiSoftKO out of an apartment, as Blaise and Dash had with their respective start-ups. Still, Kieran fondly remembered the days when he knew everything about his employees, including their favorite pizza toppings, so he could order it when they pulled all-nighters.

"I wouldn't change anything," he added.

He had all he ever wanted.

Well, almost.

Only love is missing.

He fought the urge to grimace. Love was on his mind only because of the garter he'd caught and his friends filling his head with foolish notions about his perfect woman.

Eyes bright, Selah leaned forward. "Tell me about your project."

Kieran opened his mouth and closed it. He was usually quicker under pressure, but he hadn't a clue what to say.

"If you want me to sign an NDA, I will," she offered.

His chest tightened.

Selah wasn't only a beautiful woman. She was also sharp and had integrity.

"It's not that." A bitterness coated his mouth, making him want to start over to when they met and ask for her number before she left Mason's office. He glanced at the cup on his desk. "I haven't had enough caffeine this morning, so my synapses aren't firing normally."

"I've had two myself." A slight pink colored her cheeks. "I would be on my third if I hadn't driven over here."

A mutual affection for caffeine gave them something in common. Kieran had gone out with women with less. "Glad I'm not alone in being fueled by…"

"Arabica," they said at the same time.

He realized he'd found someone who enjoyed coffee as much as him. "Unless you need the caffeine, then it's…"

"Robusta." With a laugh, she raised her hand. "Coffeeholic."

He lifted his hand. "Same, though I prefer Javaphile."

"That's a good one." Her eyes lit up. "A perk when TVT started doing well was that the cafeteria started serving a better coffee brand. Our new headquarters has full-time baristas. It's heaven."

He'd found a kindred spirit. "We have coffee carts, but now you've got me thinking I should upgrade."

"I would."

Kieran wasn't sure if she was joking or serious. Perhaps a combination. Until he remembered why she was here. "Mason speaks highly of you."

"That's my boss for you."

"It isn't false praise."

"No, it isn't." Her tone was too genuine to be boastful.

"I have project managing down to a science, and he enjoys showing off his assets to his friends."

Mason did that with his yachts and one-of-a-kind cars, but Kieran hadn't expected Selah to lump herself in with her boss's collectibles. "Does that bother you?"

Her expression didn't change. "No, given my contributions to TVT and how long I've known him, I am an asset. Highly paid and treated well for said contributions."

Confident. Kieran liked that.

Who was he kidding? He'd liked everything about Selah Burton when they'd met. He remained captivated by her today.

However, there was a problem—a big one.

Tell her the truth.

Kieran should. His gut told him to be honest, but she might not find his friends' matchmaking efforts humorous, especially with her boss involved. It might be better to tell her a version of the truth and save the rest for later. "I wasn't expecting you today. Mason texted me you were on your way right before you arrived, so you've caught me unprepared."

Understatement of the year.

"I'm sorry." He ignored the knots forming in his stomach. "You drove over here, and I'm not ready."

"Oh." Selah dragged her upper teeth over her lower lip before reaching into the bag and pulling out a business card. She handed it to him. "It's not a problem. This is nothing new with Mason. He slams his foot against the pedal when he needs to ease up on the accelerator. My work and cell numbers are on the card. Contact me when you're ready."

"Saturday." Once again, the word burst from Kieran's mouth. "We could have brunch and go over…things."

Surely by the weekend he would figure out a project for them to work on together.

She placed her bag on her lap. "That sounds fine."

Kieran released the breath he hadn't realized he'd been holding.

"Great." Now he needed to think of the perfect place for their date—er, meeting. "I'll text you details."

"Sounds good." Selah looked like she wanted to say more.

"What?"

She reached into her bag again. "TVT uses your business suite of products."

Kieran nodded. His friends who'd settled in the Pacific Northwest with its Silicon Forest instead of the Bay Area's Silicon Valley had supported his company in the best possible way.

"I've used them for years." Selah handed him a few sheets of paper. "I'm not sure when you plan another update. The last one was decent, but here are items to consider fixing when you do the next one."

As his blood pressure spiraled into the red zone, his posture went rigid. "Fixing" implied something was broken, and that *wasn't* possible.

Kieran started to speak but stopped when he remembered he'd learned more from his company's critics than his fans. He would listen before telling her she was wrong. He scanned the first page, trying to keep his mouth from gaping. The amount of detail was borderline obsessive. They'd hired expensive consulting firms and received less information.

His fingers crinkled the edges of the papers, so he loosened his grip on them. "Did your team put this together?"

"I did." She lifted her chin a notch. "Mason mentioned you were number two in the sector. This might explain why."

Kieran flinched. She'd shot an arrow at his heart with bullseye precision. But he wasn't arrogant enough to discount her findings. He continued reading, amazed his developers and the quality assurance team hadn't noticed some of these things.

That he, the developer and founder, hadn't.

"Does it make sense?" she asked, her words slightly rushed.

"Yes." Kieran flipped to the next page. He needed more time to review the list in-depth, but he appreciated her thoroughness. An average user wouldn't notice many items. Some he would call personal preferences, so they weren't a big deal, but a few…

Only a person with a highly technical background—most likely obsessive about their processes—would see a problem.

Kieran recognized quick fixes on some. Others would take longer, and two weren't worth doing. But seeing DigiSoftKO take over the number one position had been a long-time goal.

"Thank you." No one enjoyed having their mistakes

pointed out, but he appreciated she'd taken the time to do this. Her list also gave him an idea for a project. "No wonder Mason suggested you help us kick off the update to our business suite."

Selah straightened. "So, that's the project?"

Kieran nodded.

She grinned. "About time."

He made a mental note to keep her away from the development team. She might be correct, but they didn't need to hear that.

Still, a job offer perched on the tip of his tongue. She would be an asset to his company. But two things stopped him—his friendship with Mason, and Kieran wanting to go out with her.

He was attracted, mesmerized, intrigued. The list of verbs about her kept growing.

Selah was the perfect combo of beauty and brains. She also wasn't afraid to speak her mind in front of him. No wonder Mason called her his right-hand person.

Kieran couldn't wait until they met on Saturday. He wanted to get to know her better. Perhaps once he did, he would call her something, too—his girlfriend.

* * *

After Kieran saw Selah out, he grabbed his phone to see Mason's reply.

Mason: *To help you get ready to launch a big project.*
Mason: *Hope you have one for her.*

Forget messaging. Instead, he called Mason. Kieran wanted an explanation—answers—faster than a text would provide. He hit call.

On the second ring, the line connected.

"How did it go?" The words rushed out.

"It went fine, no thanks to you." Kieran breathed in through his nose and exhaled through his mouth to keep himself calm. "This situation has Henry written all over it, but I thought better of you."

"It was my idea. I was having coffee with…" Mason paused. "It came to me in a stroke of brilliance on Tuesday afternoon. Henry agreed this was the perfect way for you to spend time with Selah."

"Except for the project."

"Come on." Mason scoffed. "A company your size always has projects."

"Not ones important enough to steal away your friend's right-hand person."

"This will drastically increase my workload, but what are friends for?"

Kieran wasn't buying that for a minute. "You want to win the bet."

"That, too." Mason sounded as if he were smiling. "So, did you come up with a project for her?"

"Yes, after Selah told me what's wrong with our top-selling software."

Mason sucked in a breath. "I asked her not to ice-pick-you-in-the-forehead with her list."

Kieran almost laughed. He could imagine Selah doing that. Surprisingly, it didn't turn him off. He appreciated her honesty—found it refreshing. Though based on what Mason said, she'd bit her tongue. Kieran wouldn't mind seeing her unleash. "She didn't."

"That surprises me. Selah speaks her mind."

Kieran rubbed the spot over his heart. "She made a few direct hits."

"Admit it," Mason pressed. "My plan is brilliant."

"It's dishonest."

"The means justifies the end," Mason countered. "You'll be able to get to know Selah while she helps with the project. That's multiple days in a row. That's better than asking her out to dinner."

"A successful and profitable company doesn't invent projects so its founder can meet a beautiful woman."

"You think Selah's beautiful, huh?"

"Mase—"

"This is an out-of-the-box solution to an age-old problem."

Kieran shook his head before realizing Mason couldn't see him. "You and Henry are now at the bottom of my friends' list."

"We won't be for long. Trust me."

Kieran gripped his phone. "The more you say that, the less I trust you."

"At least I gave you some warning. Henry wanted to surprise you."

Typical Henry. "Thanks for not listening to him."

"I've got you covered." Mason chuckled. "Good luck."

Kieran had a feeling he would need more than luck with Selah Burton.

Chapter Four

Saturday morning, Selah walked to meet Kieran for brunch. The downtown Portland street was quiet, even for a weekend. Only a ride-share car had driven by since she parked.

She wasn't sure why Mason was so adamant about her helping with his friend's project launch. This was way beyond the scope of her job responsibilities. Sure, he called it a favor, but he wouldn't answer her questions. If anything, Mason had avoided her for the rest of the week. That was easy for her boss to do with his busy schedule, but the few times she'd seen him, he appeared to be distracted. She didn't understand why.

Their enormous project was on track, the stock was at an all-time high, and positive buzz about the upcoming upgrade was everywhere. Something outside of the office must be on his mind, which was none of her business. Their working relationship rarely strayed outside work.

Still, she wondered what Mason wasn't telling her. She had no idea why Kieran needed her help when he had a company full of employees. If one was unavailable, he must have others to help him. She planned on asking because he needed to make sure he had qualified people to step in whenever required.

The sun shone brightly in the cloudless sky.

Sweat beaded at her hairline. It was a good thing the restaurant wasn't far.

The temperature had risen since she left her house, only fifteen minutes ago. That meant the day would be a scorcher. Not unusual for mid-July, but she wasn't a fan of ninety degrees or higher. She didn't mind the rain or overcast skies. After growing up in Phoenix, where dry heat was still hot, there was such a thing as too much blue sky and sun.

With each step, her bag hit her hip. She'd done preliminary work last night, but the laptop bag had become her de facto purse. Even if she hadn't had things to show Kieran, the strap would be on her shoulder.

As she approached the restaurant, she slowed. No one stood on the sidewalk in front of it. The best brunch places in Portland drew a crowd, so she'd expected to see people waiting outside for a table unless the café was reservations only.

As she entered, the aroma of freshly baked goods filled the air. Her stomach growled, eager for a taste. Instrumental music played. The contemporary tune matched the decor. Brick walls, wood flooring, and natural light through the front window provided a warm and welcoming feeling. The exposed ceilings with ductwork and pipes gave off a modern vibe. The combination worked well together, and the environment would be productive for their first meeting.

A man wearing black stood behind a tall counter. "Ms. Burton?"

How does he know my name?

She glanced down to see if she'd worn her lanyard with a badge by mistake, but it wasn't there. Her gaze met his. "Yes. That's me."

"Mr. O'Neal is seated." The host stepped out into the aisle. "Please follow me."

She did, passing empty tables. That was odder than no one waiting outside. This was prime brunch time, and Mason had mentioned this place to her. It was popular.

So where was everybody?

The host led her to a square table with two chairs on each side. Large, but the area was secluded. He pulled out a chair for her. "Enjoy."

"Hey." Kieran stood. He wore khakis with a navy polo shirt. The front of his hair had fallen over his forehead, making him appear younger—carefree.

Her pulse kicked up a notch.

The casual style suited him. Call her old-fashioned, but his manners appealed to her at a gut level. She'd noticed them in Mason's office on Tuesday. "Hi."

"Did you find the place okay?"

Selah nodded before removing the strap from her shoulder. "I've never been here, but Mason loves it."

"My friends and I eat here a lot."

"I can see why." She placed her bag on an empty chair and sat. "Comfy atmosphere."

"Yes. But wait until you taste the food." Kieran took his seat and filled her cup with a carafe from the table. "I ordered coffee."

"Thanks." She didn't need the caffeine this morning, but she wouldn't turn down a cup. "The restaurant is quiet for a Saturday brunch."

A sheepish expression crossed his face.

Mason often looked the same way. That meant… "What did you do?"

"I reserved the entire place."

Her lips parted. "Why?"

"So, we could talk without having to deal with noise."

A billionaire's thought process differed from others, but Kieran appeared more…grounded than her boss.

As if I know much about him.

She nearly snorted. Her imagination was getting the best of her.

Uh-oh. Selah had done the same thing with Axel. She shouldn't think of Kieran as anything other than her temporary part-time boss. Her heart was off-limits to all men, including good-looking billionaires with manners. "That will make working easier."

He glanced at the chair with her laptop bag. "You came prepared."

"I did, but in full transparency, I rarely leave home without my laptop." As she patted it, the feel of her planner brought relief. She preferred having that with her at all times, too. "It's a bad habit. Though having my computer with me comes in handy when Mason needs something, and I'm not at home."

"I'm sure it does." Kieran took a sip of his coffee. "But since we're both working on a day off, let's eat first, and we can work after our meal."

"Okay." She assumed they'd talk about work while they ate, but she was flexible. The truth was, she usually worked on the weekends.

Selah raised her cup. The aroma of the coffee swirled in front of her nose, making her mouth water. She took a sip. The dark blend was potent and perfect. "Excellent."

He drank again. "One of my favorites."

"I can see why." She placed the drink on the table before picking up the menu. "Any suggestions?"

Kieran hadn't picked up his menu. "Everything is delicious, but if you enjoy coffee cake, be sure to order a slice on the side. It's a breakfast specialty."

"That must be what I smelled baking when I entered."

He nodded. "If you want to try more than one thing, we can order the chef's choice, which consists of smaller versions of their larger entrees. That's what I usually get."

"I'm game. As long as they include the coffee cake."

"They will." His face lit up.

Her heart bumped. She lowered her gaze to the menu in front of her.

No. No. No.

Her heart was not allowed to bump or pound or anything in between.

So what if they enjoyed a good cup of coffee and coffee cake? That meant nothing.

Focus. She needed to focus on why she was here and be

polite. "How was your week?"

"Busy as usual. Yours?"

"Same." She clutched her cup. "The dates on the calendar change, but that's about it."

"I know the feeling." He shifted in his chair. "Mason has mentioned you a few times, but nothing specific. How did you end up working at TVT?"

Mason kept his personal life private, which was what she preferred. He'd known about her and Axel only because she'd wanted to give him a heads-up and make sure dating Axel was okay. Mason had been all for the relationship until he found out what Axel had done. Thankfully, Axel's contract position ended shortly after that. It hadn't been renewed because the project was finished.

But she would never date someone she worked with again.

Lesson learned.

She washed away the terrible memories with a swig of coffee. "I was Mason's TA."

"In college?"

Nodding, she laughed, remembering when they met. "He was a sophomore taking a higher-level CS course. Most students would have been intimidated, but he breezed into the classroom as if he were the professor."

"Did he get an A?"

"He did." Not everyone had gotten along with Mason. He was a jokester and arrogant, thinking he was the smartest person in the room. Most of the time, he was but not always. When that happened, it was difficult for him to see another path or solution once he set his mind on something. More than a few classmates were jealous. "I needed help with my research, and he volunteered. That led to us brainstorming ideas that would later evolve into TVT."

Kieran leaned forward. "You were involved from the beginning?"

"Before TVT was anything." She'd thought Mason's idea had merit, but not even he'd foreseen what a success it would be. "Officially, I'm employee number two."

Kieran's head tilted. "I had no idea you and Mason had worked together for so long."

"He was nineteen when we met." She remembered the only negative part of accepting his job offer. "I dropped out of grad school to work with him. My parents haven't forgiven me. Even though I bought them a vacation home, my mom and dad still believe I made a mistake."

"I'm sorry."

She shrugged. "It's their problem, not mine. I have zero regrets."

"Given Mason's cut, I'm assuming you did well."

"Yes, but I'm not ready to retire or switch companies."

"You sound certain."

She raised her chin. "I am. I enjoy my job and have plenty of money. Mason has a million ideas, so I'm never bored."

"He said you're a product manager."

Of course, Mason did because that was what she did for him—manage his products. He also hadn't made the organizational chart, or everyone would be listed by their first names and whatever they wanted to be called. "I'm Chief Product Officer."

Kieran's mouth gaped. He closed it. "So, you helping me…"

"Should tell you how much your friend wants to help you."

He started to speak but stopped. Gratitude shone in his eyes. "Thank you."

"Happy to help." No matter what her parents thought about her job, Selah owed Mason. Even if she complained, she would do whatever favor he needed. But she wouldn't mention that to Kieran. She didn't want the info to reach her boss, or Mason would take advantage of that. It was his nature. "So, tell me how you got the idea for your company."

"You mean my boring business software as my friends call it," he teased. "Unlike their sexier, cutting edge technologies and products."

"Someone has to make the practical stuff."

"Practical is better than boring. And that person is me." He refilled his coffee cup. "But the reason DigiSoftKO exists is because of my mom."

Selah hadn't expected him to say that. "Your mom?"

"She raised my brother, sister, and me on her own. She worked as a secretary and took pride in her job. But one time, she had issues with the company's spreadsheet software, missed completing a report by the deadline, and was fired."

"That's a harsh punishment."

"It was ridiculous because the problems weren't her fault. The program manufacturer admitted as much after I did some digging. But the company wouldn't rehire her. They'd wanted to downsize, and this gave them a reason to cut her position." Lines deepened on his forehead, matching the severe tone of his voice. "It spurred me to create something better, so no other single moms lost their jobs because of a software issue."

"Wow, I shouldn't have given you my list the other day."

"Don't be sorry." He laughed. "You should have seen what my mom wanted to be changed when she beta-tested the program."

"Your mom sounds like a smart woman."

"Very. She retired five years ago, and we all miss her."

Wait. What? "Your mom worked for you?"

"Yes, and trust me, no nepotism was involved. My mom kept us going in the beginning. She put in as many hours as I did."

Selah tried to imagine her mom working at TVT—tried and failed. Her academic mother wouldn't have lasted a day at the startup, then or now. She preferred research over everything, including parenting. One time, Selah had gone to see her mom during office hours to talk to her because she was never home. That hadn't gone over well.

"That's great it worked out." A part of her was envious.

"Yes." His mouth curved at the corners. "But she was ready to retire. For her going-away present, I bought her old company and let her decide what to do with the assets. Her new job is being 'Nana' to my sister's kids, and she is so happy."

The affection in his voice was palpable. That told Selah

one thing. "You're close to your family."

"As one can be with a crazy work schedule." He sipped his coffee, but his smile never wavered. "We talk more than we see each other in person, but that's okay for now. It's always been us against the world. That hasn't changed. I hope it never does."

"If you've lasted this long, the odds are good it won't." Selah couldn't remember feeling this comfortable with a stranger.

A server dressed in black with her hair in a high ponytail came to the table. "Are you ready to order, or will you be having the usual, Kieran?"

Selah found it interesting the server knew Kieran so well.

He nodded. "The chef's choice and coffee cake."

The server laughed. "So, the usual."

Kieran handed her the menus. "Creature of habit."

"Not really." The server's curious gaze traveled to Selah. "You're not here with the guys."

Selah waited for him to say this was a working meeting.

Instead, he grinned as if keeping a secret. "I'm not."

"About time." The server studied Selah for a moment before checking the carafe. "I'll bring you more coffee."

With that, she walked away.

Selah sipped her drink. "You come here a lot."

He nodded. "But I've never brought a date."

Date? Her muscles tensed, and each nerve ending shrieked. "This isn't…"

"Or someone for a meeting." The words rushed out. His eyes clouded with what appeared to be concern. "I hope I haven't made you uncomfortable."

The sincerity in his voice sent a sigh of relief to her lips. "No, and sorry if I overreacted. It's a touchy subject for me. I dated a contract employee who worked at TVT. After that disaster, I promised myself I'd never break that rule again."

His gaze narrowed. "I didn't realize TVT has a fraternization policy."

The memory of Axel's betrayal and her hurt brought a shudder. "It's not a company rule but a personal one."

Kieran appeared to want to say something, but he sipped before lowering his cup. "Then, it's a good thing this isn't a date."

His tone was harsher than usual. His coffee must have gone down wrong. Still, Selah was glad he understood. And why wouldn't he?

It wasn't as if someone like him would date a woman like her. She was an organizer and manager, a woman who got things done, not one who men dreamed of dating, especially a billionaire.

For the best.

Which logically made sense after Axel. She only wished her heart agreed.

Chapter Five

Sunday night, Kieran paced the length of his penthouse loft. His bare feet preferred the soft rug to the hardwood floor, but that didn't stop him. He quickened his steps, needing to do something other than eying his cell phone on the coffee table.

The silence mocked him.

He rarely paid attention to his notifications or calls, but he'd had zero in the past twenty-four hours. His friends kept busy during the weekend, so that wasn't surprising. Some headed to vacation homes in Hood Hamlet. If people were in town, they met for brunch or to watch games if any were scheduled. If not, it was a time to rest, sleep in, kick back, or catch up.

Only Kieran didn't want to do any of those things.

He wanted Mason to return his texts and calls.

Come on, phone. Ring.

Of course, it didn't.

After saying goodbye to Selah, Kieran had texted Mason several times yesterday and hadn't received a reply. This morning, Kieran had called—something he rarely did and left a message. Again, no response. That wasn't like Mason. He must be dealing with a crisis at TVT, but Mason could type a one-word text. So where was he?

The cell phone rang.

The sound startled Kieran, but a glance at the screen showed Mason's name.

Finally. Kieran placed the phone against his ear. "Where have you been?"

"Whoa. Slow down, digital cowboy. Only my mom is allowed to ask that question."

"I've been trying to reach you since yesterday."

"You've been blowing up my phone." Silence filled the line. "What's going on?"

"I saw Selah yesterday."

"And…"

"You and Henry have completely messed up my chances with her. She won't go out with someone she works with, and since she's working on a project for my company that includes me."

"Sorry, dude. I had no idea she had that rule." Mason sounded sincere. "Guess she learned her lesson after Axel. Good for her."

"Not for me. We worked at the restaurant. It was…"

"Productive."

"Yes, but awkward. I don't want to work with her. I want to take her out."

Kiss her.

Kieran had never wanted to kiss anyone as much as he

wanted to kiss Selah. She was beautiful and intelligent and spoke her mind. He hadn't believed the perfect woman existed, but now he kept thinking he'd found her. "I don't know what to do."

Which was unlike him.

Mason laughed. "A good thing you have me."

"What do I do?"

"Fire her." Mason spoke in a matter-of-fact tone.

"What?" Kieran yelled.

"Keep it down, or you'll burst my eardrum."

"I can't fire her."

"Don't be so literal," Mason sighed. "Tell Selah the project's canceled or postponed. It's not like she's getting paid for this."

"You're paying her salary."

"Which she earns whether or not she's helping you. I don't see the issue."

"I've been dishonest. So have you."

"She never has to know."

"But I want to go ahead with the project. She's brilliant. Her suggestions—"

Mason growled. "You try to hire her away from me, and you'll regret the day you were born."

"If she worked for me, I'd never be able to date her. As it is—"

"Stop making things so complicated." Mason cut him off. "If you don't want to fire her, get her input on the project, let her set up the process, and after that's finished, ask her out."

"I'd rather not wait."

"You can't always have everything you want when you want it."

"Not true, and you know that."

"Okay, I concede that point, but there are rare instances when having billions of dollars won't help you. This situation with Selah is one of those times."

"Asking her out on a date would have been easier."

"Too late." Mason blew out a breath. "You'll have to be patient. Did you speak with Henry?"

"He was no help."

"What did he tell you to do?"

"Kidnap Selah, fly to Las Vegas, and ask her to marry me on the steps of a twenty-four-hour wedding chapel."

"Don't you dare elope." The words rushed out. "You need to hire the Posh Planner for your wedding."

Huh? Mason wasn't making sense. "First, no wedding is happening, but who?"

"The event planner who coordinated Adam and Cambria's wedding. Rachael's excellent at what she does."

"If I ever get married, I'll remember that."

"Not if, when. You caught the garter."

Kieran shook his head. "You sound like Henry."

"I'll take that as a compliment."

"You would."

Mason's yawn sounded through the phone. "Long day. I need to go."

"Work?"

He hesitated. "A side project I have going."

"Get some sleep."

"And, Kieran?"

"Yes?"

"You're frustrated, but trust me, Selah is worth waiting for."

"She is." Kieran gripped his phone. But if she met another man before she finished working on the launch, he would never forgive Henry and Mason.

* * *

This was a mistake.

As Selah headed toward Kieran's office on Monday morning, she fought the urge to turn around. The project might be necessary, but spending more time with Kieran wasn't smart. Not when she hadn't been able to stop thinking about him all weekend. Okay, not *all*. Only from the time they'd said goodbye in front of the restaurant on Saturday afternoon.

Pathetic.

Hadn't she learned her lesson about pretty boys?

And this one was a billionaire. That spelled double-trouble, given what she'd figured out from her boss.

The less time she spent with Kieran, the better.

That gave her an idea. One that had been gelling since yesterday.

It should accomplish what she needed to happen to survive this assignment without a massive crush developing.

As long as Kieran agreed.

Selah crossed her fingers.

His assistant wasn't sitting at the desk outside his office, but the door was ajar. She knocked, pushing it open farther. "Kieran?"

"Come in."

She did.

He stood behind his desk, looking sweeter than a caramel macchiato in his tailored suit, crisp shirt, and tie. "Good morning."

"Hey—hi." Okay, not the most eloquent response, but the way his hair fell over his forehead made it hard to think. Add in a tongue two sizes too big, and the pathway from her brain to her mouth wasn't functioning correctly. "Enjoy the rest of your weekend?"

"I did. You?"

"I worked."

"Get caught up?"

"I got ahead." Because of having to be here. Might as well see if he would go for her plan. "Which gave me an idea."

Kieran motioned to a chair, and she sat. So did he.

"You're overseeing this project, but you don't have the time or a reason to learn what I do. Your project managers are the ones who need to understand so they can implement the process in the future." Selah waited for him to respond. He didn't. "I suggest I work directly with them and report back to you."

A beat passed and another.

Then a bright smile that would make a supernova appear

dull lit up his face. "That's a great idea. Please keep me in the loop."

Thank goodness. She released the breath she'd been holding. "I will."

"Does that mean you want to meet with the product managers alone this morning?"

Her plan would work. Selah nodded, ignoring the twinkle in his eyes. "The email you sent with the invitation explains why I'm here."

"It does." He studied her as if trying to debug a line of code. "I'll send another email to make sure everyone understands."

That sounded like overkill to her. But Kieran knew his people.

He straightened a stack of papers that appeared to be perfectly aligned already. "I wish I had the time to follow along. I'm sure you could teach everyone here a few things."

He's being polite. The compliment means nothing. Still, she stood taller. "I wouldn't go that far, but thanks."

Her gaze met his. Those ridiculously long eyelashes of his were to-die-for. But she couldn't look away.

Kieran blinked, breaking whatever connected them. "Check-in before you leave."

Not wanting to stare at him a nanosecond longer, Selah glanced at his tidy desk. Even his pen was placed perpendicular to the edge. She, however, was entirely out of alignment.

She cleared her throat. "I will."

His Adam's apple bobbed. "Anything else?"

He appeared impatient. Of course, he did. She was supposed to be here working, not making goo-goo eyes at him. She raised her chin. "No."

As Selah walked out of the office, she clutched her laptop's strap hanging off her shoulder.

Don't look back.

Even if she were tempted, she…wouldn't. The way he dismissed her was so boss-like. He had better things to do, which told her what she'd already known. The connection had been in her mind. The attraction between them was one-sided—hers.

And though that was disappointing, it was probably for the best.

Wait. Not probably.

For the best.

* * *

Kieran lost himself in his work. Only this morning, that took effort because his gaze kept straying to the time. Now that eleven o'clock was approaching, he wanted to go to the conference room where Selah was. *Nope. Not going to do it.* Keeping his butt in his chair was the smartest—the only— option today.

Yes, he wanted to see Selah. Something about her was…addictive. But her plan to work with his employees meant he didn't waste time he didn't have.

Kieran blinked before refocusing on the email on his screen.

Unfortunately, the upcoming meeting's agenda didn't interest him. Not as much as remembering the sheen in her hair from the overhead lighting. Her black pants and white blouse were stylish and the definition of business casual, but if she wore a floral wreath, an ethereal gown, and wings instead, she could easily be mistaken for a fairy. She'd put him under a spell. No wand required.

At this rate, he would get nothing done.

Not good.

A knock sounded.

He glanced at the door. "Come in."

Selah entered. Her trusty laptop bag hung from her shoulder.

Kieran stood. "Hey."

Her smile shot straight into his heart. "I'm finished for the day."

She would likely work another eight at TVT. And that was one hundred percent his fault. He tugged at his tie to loosen it. "How'd it go?"

"Great." Her tone was cheerful, which reaffirmed how much she enjoyed what she did. "I left your product managers with homework. It shouldn't take them too long."

"I have confidence they'll rise to the task."

"I'm sure they will. Your people catch on quickly. I doubt this project setup will take long."

The sooner he no longer worked with her, the sooner he could ask her out. "Great."

Her gaze met his. Her lips parted as if inviting him to taste.

Oh, man. Kieran wanted to, but his desk kept him from leaning in to take what he wanted.

A good thing.

One thing he'd learned that had helped him become a billionaire was patience. He would rely on that now because he wouldn't blow his shot with Selah.

The fluttery feeling told him if Kieran did, he would regret it for a very long time. "So I'll see you tomorrow."

"Bright and early."

Not early enough for him. Selah hadn't left, but he missed her. "Don't work too hard."

"I'd say the same to you, but you wouldn't listen."

Not true. But only because she said it. "Lesson learned from Mason?"

She nodded. "Have a great rest of your day."

With that, she left his office.

As soon as Kieran could no longer see her, he rested his forehead against his desk. Henry and Mason needed to pay for putting him through this.

The only question—how much should it cost them?

Chapter Six

On Tuesday, Kieran spoke to Selah for less than five minutes. It wasn't nearly long enough. More than once, he'd been tempted to walk by the conference room, but he didn't want to be a distraction. Besides, he had a ton of work to do himself. He focused on the recap of quarterly financials.

A knock sounded.

He glanced at the closed door. "It's open."

Selah walked in, and his heart thudded. "Things went well this morning."

Kieran stood, fighting the urge to comb his fingers through his hair and straighten his tie. "Excellent."

She dragged her upper teeth over her lower lip. "People spoke more openly today than yesterday."

Her tone held a warning that gave him pause. "About?"

"A few have issues about the project management software."

Wait. What? A tension formed between his shoulder blades. "What issues?"

"Some were the same as mine. I emailed a list to you. No one was negative. It was more…constructive criticism."

Or was she trying to soften the critics?

He pulled up his inbox and opened her email. As he read, tension turned into knots. "Why didn't they speak up?"

Selah shrugged. "Fear. At least two told their manager or supervisor, who thought their concerns weren't a big deal."

Kieran stiffened. "It's a big deal to me. I care what they think."

"Tell them that," she encouraged in a kind tone that made him want to hug her.

"I thought I had, but we've been so busy they might have forgotten."

"Hey." As she leaned over his desk, a whiff of vanilla and sandalwood tickled his nose. "You're an excellent CEO. Let your people know their opinions matter to you. Mason has a special email address for employee suggestions. If someone wishes to remain anonymous, there's a suggestion box in the food court with pen and paper available. Totally old school, but he receives notes each week."

"Your idea." It wasn't a question.

She grinned wryly. "Perhaps."

That meant yes. Kieran almost laughed. "I'll get my assistant on it. Thanks."

She glanced at her phone.

"Do you have time to grab a cup of coffee or an early lunch?" he asked.

"I need to get to TVT, but I would like to meet later this

week to review where things stand."

"Thursday." The word flew from his lips. That would be sooner than Friday. "My day is booked, but I'm free that evening. We could talk over dinner."

Selah hesitated.

The wariness in her gaze bugged him. "Here at my office," he added to put her at ease. "I'll have food delivered."

The tight lines around her mouth relaxed. She checked her phone. "I'm free after five-thirty."

"I'll mark it down. Any food allergies?"

"None." She typed on her screen.

"Be sure to pop in tomorrow and update me on how the project planning is going."

"I will." Selah lowered her cell phone. "You'll be pleased once it's all set up."

"I'm sure I will be." Especially since he could ask her out for real.

* * *

On Wednesday morning, Selah met with Kieran's product team again. The people were quick learners who asked intelligent questions and did what she assigned them. The launch plan was coming together. Slower than she would have completed it. But this way, Kieran's company would be set for the future. And Mason would stop bugging her.

As her gaze traveled around the room, she closed her laptop. Her boss didn't call her the master of multitasking for nothing. "I'll see you tomorrow. Let me know if you have questions."

People filed out of the room, eager to get to their actual jobs or lunch. She slid her computer into its case.

"It looks as if things are progressing well."

Selah's hand flew to her chest before she glanced to the doorway.

Kieran leaned against the doorjamb. The casual pose was a stark contrast to his suit and tie. But boy, the guy was attractive.

A warning bell sounded. She could almost hear a robotic voice yelling, "danger, danger."

"Yes." Her gaze returned to her bag. "Your team picks up things quickly. We should be done next week."

"You work fast."

"Fast is good as long as you're thorough." She stood, not liking him having the height advantage, even though he was at least ten feet away. Something about him unsettled her. She hated being flustered, but that was how she felt whenever Kieran O'Neal was around. She gave him a brief recap of what they did today. "Do you have questions?"

"No."

"I'll get—"

"Have lunch with me."

But Kieran said he had no questions. "Why?"

"You need to eat." The words rushed from his mouth. "Mason says you skip meals."

"More like I forget, but I catch up." She motioned to herself. "As you can tell, I'm far from being on the thin side."

"You're perfect." His face reddened. "I mean, you're fine. For your height. Bone structure. I should probably stop now."

Selah laughed. Perhaps she wasn't the only one who got flustered when they were together, though she doubted it was for the same reason. Still, his actions made Kieran appear more approachable. Not that he hadn't been around her, but she'd felt…off. Through Mason, she'd met a few billionaires, and oddly enough, they were more down to earth than she expected.

Well, not Henry.

But Mason said his friend was in a league of his own.

"So lunch?" Kieran asked.

She glanced at the time.

"It can be quick," he said before she replied. "I don't want to send you to TVT with an empty stomach."

That was sweet. "As long as it's fast."

"Like lightning. Except not so fast either of us chokes." His Adam's apple bobbed. "We can take things slower tomorrow night."

Dinner. She hadn't forgotten. If anything, she'd been looking forward to it. For work purposes only. If she kept repeating that, she might believe it. "But you must be busy. We could talk fast today."

"Fast isn't always the best." Kieran straightened. "Let's have lunch, and you can tell me how our food compares to TVTs."

Selah half laughed. "Do you and Mason compete with everything?"

"Me, Mason, and Blaise usually do. Adam and Henry don't care. Dash is usually lost in his thoughts. And Brett is too busy staring at his daughter's latest photos."

She was familiar with all the names thanks to her boss. "What will you do if TVT's food is better?"

He shrugged, but the last thing he felt was indifference. "Hire your chef."

"Mason wouldn't like that."

"He would get over it. Now, if I hired you, Mason might kill me."

"Yes, he would." She raised her chin. "Not that you could afford me."

* * *

Having lunch with Kieran when they were meeting for dinner tomorrow night made little sense to Selah. Yes, Mason worried about her, even though he was as apt to skip a meal. A part of her wondered if her temporary boss wanted to spend more time with her. And the idea didn't upset her as much as it should.

Who was she kidding?

Kieran's interest flattered Selah. Of course, she might be imagining things. Still, he stared at her.

A lot.

She'd caught him on at least seven occasions. Not that she was counting. Okay, she was. But each time made her…wonder.

Yesterday, Selah had worried she'd drawn a weird shape

on her face with her pen. But nothing was there when she glanced in her rearview mirror. No food stuck in between her teeth, either.

The attention might have nothing to do with her and was how Kieran acted. He might focus on whomever he spoke with. That must be the case because sitting here in his company's cafeteria, which reminded her of a high-end mall food court with better meal options, was what he'd said it would be—lunch and a mini food tasting.

Selah shook off the disappointment.

For the best.

That was becoming her new catchphrase. One that was bugging her.

Not that she was about to change it.

She wouldn't get involved with someone she worked with, not even temporarily. So what if months had passed since she'd felt the inkling of wanting to date anyone? She'd put Axel behind her and moved forward. Being attracted to someone—okay, Kieran—had to be a sign she was on the right track. She would find someone else to fall for soon.

Probably as soon as this project ended.

That would be…good.

Kieran sat across the table from her. He leaned forward. "How does the food compare to what's served at TVT?"

Selah wiped her mouth with a napkin. "Your mac and cheese is better—my compliments to the chef. But the French fries don't come close to ours. Yours must use a healthier oil for deep frying."

"TVT doesn't?"

She shook her head. "Mason is maniacal over fries and made the kitchen change oils until he found one he preferred. And it's not as healthy as the first they tried."

Kieran laughed. "I suspected Mason had a diva side. No wonder he gets along with Henry so well."

"In my boss's defense, he considers French fries a food group. A dozen different dipping sauces are offered in the cafeteria, too."

"That explains why he got us all a set of fry sauces before football season began last fall. Though I must admit, a couple were out of this world."

"One of his investments." It wasn't a secret, since Mason's name was on the website. "Adam bought his whiskey distillery around the same time."

"Mason mentioned a food investment, but I thought he meant a brewpub or restaurant."

Selah tried the tossed green salad with cranberries, nuts, and feta cheese. *Not bad.* The light vinaigrette was delicious. She wiped her mouth. "He might own one of those, too. I lost track, and he only mentions stuff like that in passing."

"That doesn't sound like Mason. He enjoys bragging."

"To his friends. Not his employees."

Kieran studied her with an assessing gaze.

"What?" she asked.

"Did Mason give you a set of fry sauce?"

"Everyone at TVT got one. I'm sure the reorders turned that gift into a very successful loss leader for him." She half laughed. "It's as if each Billionaire of Silicon Forest has the Midas touch."

"Dash Cabot is the Midas of our group, but we haven't done badly."

"You've all done extremely well."

"Once you experience a big success, future ones don't seem as out of reach as they once were."

"That makes sense."

"Have you made any fun investments?" he asked.

"Not really. I've sold a little company stock, and my life is pretty much work, but I support a local animal rescue. I enjoy volunteering there and have done that for years, so donating has been another way to help besides being there a couple of hours a week."

"Do you have any pets?"

"No, but I get my fill when I'm there." Still, that didn't ease the longing in her gut. "Someday, when I no longer work so many hours, I'll get two cats or a dog and a cat, but those are a ways off."

"Mason needs you."

She laughed. "Yes. There's more to do and accomplish at TVT."

"You're loyal."

"Yes, but thanks to Mason, that feeling runs through the entire company."

"You'd never consider resigning?"

"Nope." She didn't hesitate to answer. "I love what I do. And I believe in TVT's products. When it's time to start a family or if I get bored, I'll feel differently, but who knows when that'll happen?"

He inhaled sharply. "True."

"How about you? Do you plan on staying here?"

"Like you, I have no reason to leave. I'm proud of what I've built. But you never know what the future will hold. So until there's something else I want to do, I'm staying put."

Chapter Seven

Thursday night, Kieran double-checked the table where he planned to eat with Selah. His assistant had moved the pile of folders, papers, and computer logs to her desk. She was in the lobby waiting for Selah and dinner to arrive.

He glanced at his watch. If both were on time—the food would be because Dash's housekeeper Iris was never late—that should be any minute.

A knock sounded.

He adjusted his tie. "Come in."

Selah walked into his office with the laptop bag hanging from her shoulder. Her pink shirt and the plaid scarf tied around her neck complemented her complexion perfectly. She wore a loose ponytail, but strands of hair framed her face. She was…gorgeous.

Not a date.

Even if Kieran wished it were.

She greeted him with a smile. "Hey."

"Hello." Kieran wanted to reach out and touch her, but he remained where he was.

Selah motioned to the table. "I didn't realize you used that for anything but storage."

"Thank my assistant. Otherwise, we'd be eating on our laps."

"It wouldn't be the first time."

Another knock sounded.

"That must be our dinner." He grabbed two thermal totes and a bag from his assistant, Dora. "Thanks for staying late tonight. Don't come in until ten tomorrow."

Dora grinned. "I won't. Thanks, boss."

By the time he closed the door, Selah had her laptop set up on the table.

All work and no play…

"Let's eat first." Kieran wanted time without the project being the topic of conversation. "We have finger food, so this will save your laptop."

She shut the top. "What's for dinner?"

"You'll see. There's water or iced tea to drink." Kieran removed the plates, napkins, and forks from the bag, the bottled drinks from the smaller tote, and foil containers with plastic lids from the larger tote. "We have chips, guacamole, and *ceviche* to start. And tacos for the main course. There are fish, shrimp, chicken, and carne asada tacos."

Her eyes widened. "How will I choose?"

The excitement in her voice pleased him. He'd asked Mason about her favorite food. A good thing because he would have never come up with this on his own. Though the *ceviche* was his idea, Iris agreed it would be a nice touch, especially if his coworkers liked seafood.

He hadn't corrected her that only a single coworker—a special one—was joining him for dinner.

"You don't have to choose." He kept opening containers. The scents of spices and meat made his mouth water. Iris had outdone herself once again. "There are plenty of each."

"Guess you can never have too many tacos."

He handed her a plate. "Help yourself."

Selah did, filling her plate until she couldn't fit anything else on it. "Tacos are my favorite."

Kieran caught himself before saying *I know*. He wished she eyed him the way she did her plate. "Enjoy them."

As she sat at the other end of the table, her eyes twinkled. "I will."

He filled his plate and sat across from her. "Good?"

Chewing, she nodded. Selah wiped her mouth with a napkin. "You have to give me the name of where you ordered these from."

"Dash's housekeeper, Iris, made them. She caters events for his friends, so I asked if she minded making our dinner."

"It's delicious." She appeared to be so relaxed. "If I were you, I'd offer Iris a job and have her make tacos every day."

He would buy Selah tacos every single day if that kept a wide smile on her face. "We've tried luring Iris away, but she and Dash have been friends since middle school."

"Oh, right. Mason told me about her." Selah scooped up *ceviche* with a tortilla chip. "She does the food for his football parties."

Wait. Kieran had missed none of the Sunday gatherings

at Mason's place, but he would remember meeting Selah. "Were you there?"

She laughed. "No. I used to get consulted on what clothes Mason should wear. He's doing better now, but I sometimes hear bits and pieces after events happen."

"Does that bother you?"

"Not at all." She sounded sincere. "Mason and I work together but don't see each other outside of work unless something crops up or there's an office event. It was the same in college. We never hung out socially. I was older and his TA."

"And now he's your boss."

Nodding, she ate another chip.

Kieran wanted to ask where she drew the line or if work and her personal life overlapped at all. "Are you friends with any colleagues at TVT?"

"My closest friends work there."

So it was only Mason, and likely because he was her boss. That wouldn't be a problem for them. Well, once they finished the project launch plan.

During dinner, they spoke about their families. He showed her photos of his nieces and nephews and explained how his sister limited the type of gifts he bought them. Selah's tales about the educational "toys" she'd received as gifts from her parents made him laugh. Especially now that she collected dolls and stuffed animals—two things her mom and dad never bought her.

Kieran respected how she was more amused than bitter, understanding her parents did the best they could, even if she would have wanted board games and Barbie dolls instead. But each tidbit of information only whetted his appetite. The more he learned about her, the more he wanted to know.

She leaned back in her chair. "I may have to roll myself out of here. But it was so worth it."

He wanted to eat the brownies still in the bag, but Selah was eyeing her laptop. "Do you want to tell me how the kickoff's going?"

She opened her computer. "I made a presentation for you."

Of course, she did. He sat in the chair next to her. On second thought, this wasn't so bad.

"It's short." She clicked on the arrow to play.

As he watched the slides on the screen, the level of detail surprised him. No wonder TVT did so well with someone like her there. The graphs were on point without confusing details.

His eyes zeroed in on the end date. "You'll be finished next week?"

She nodded. "Monday if all goes right."

Anticipation shot through him. He finished watching the rest of the presentation. "I'm impressed."

Selah's eyes crinkled. "That was the reaction I hoped for. Your team is quick. They did the legwork."

"They had an excellent teacher." As he turned in his chair, his knee brushed hers. That shouldn't feel as good as it did. He had to force himself not to stay where he'd be touching her. "I can't thank you enough."

"Let me beta test the upgrade."

"That's a given."

She shimmied her shoulders. "Can't wait."

Kieran laughed. "What else do I need to know about the project kickoff?"

Selah reached into her laptop bag and pulled out a sheet of paper. "This is a one-page summary of where everyone is at."

"Mason is a lucky CEO to have you." Kieran scanned the page. "Concise."

She flushed. "Thank you. There are things executives need to know and others that would have them micromanaging. No one has time for that."

Her voice was melodic, washing over Kieran like the strumming of a harp. He swallowed around the lump in his throat. "True."

But he would make time for her. Beauty, brains, Selah was the total package.

Her gaze met his with a question in her eyes. Her pink lips parted slightly.

Did she have something to say? Or was that an invitation?

He would go with the latter.

As if pulled by a tractor beam, Kieran came closer.

Selah didn't blink. Nor did she move away. Instead, she leaned forward until her lips touched his.

Soft, spicy, home.

The kiss filled him with a sense of belonging, a sense of rightness.

He wrapped his arms around her, relishing the taste and

feel of her kiss. Holding someone had never felt more right. His lips moved over hers, pressing harder, exploring all he could. He enjoyed kissing, but with Selah, the kiss was next level.

Her arm slid over his shoulders and her fingers toyed with the ends of his hair.

As his temperature rose, his control slipped a notch. Ending the kiss was the last thing he wanted to do, but he needed to before things went further. Slowly, trying to linger as long as he could, he drew away.

Selah's breathing was ragged. Her flush deepened, and her pupils were wide. She touched her lips with two fingers.

"Wow." That was the only way to describe the kiss. Perfect was another. "I had a feeling we'd have chemistry, but that was—"

"A mistake." Her mouth tightened, and she scooted away from him. "I'm—"

"It wasn't a mistake. It was perfect."

She stood. "The kiss should have never happened."

"But it did, and I'm glad. We did nothing wrong."

Selah wouldn't look at Kieran. "You didn't, but I did."

"I've wanted to ask you out since we met. And now, we can date."

"I can't." She wiped her mouth as if she could erase their kiss.

He reached for her hand, but she jerked hers away. "Please—"

"I'll meet with the team via video conference to finish up the project. I won't be returning."

Selah didn't put her laptop into her bag. She gathered her things in her arms and ran out of his office.

As Kieran's lips tingled, he stared at the open door. He'd messed up, but he kissed her without thinking about it. Kissing her had been as natural as breathing. So how did he fix this? Because he'd found the perfect woman and wanted her in his life. But he didn't have a clue what to do next.

* * *

Friday, Selah disconnected from the video conference with the team from Kieran's company. She'd handed out their final tasks, answered questions, and told each person she was available if they needed help to finish up. She waited for the knot in her stomach to loosen.

It didn't.

She rubbed her tired eyes. She'd tossed and turned last night, unable to stop thinking about kissing Kieran. Even now, her lips wanted another one.

Knowing he wanted more kisses and to go out with her only made her feel worse. Part of her wanted that, too. But the situation felt out of control—a way she didn't want to feel after Axel.

If only she could blame Kieran for the kiss, but they were both at fault. She, more than him because of her rules— ones she gleefully ignored the moment he got close to her.

Ugh.

What had she been thinking?

Keeping things professional was the only way to go.

There were other ways to meet guys—from dating apps to professional matchmakers. She could afford it. Except Selah wanted to find a date the old-fashioned way, have lightning strike, and live happily ever after.

That was what she'd believed she found with Axel. Only he'd been as real as any book boyfriend she'd had over the years.

Pure fiction.

She yawned. Lack of sleep made her feel…off. If she went to bed early tonight, she would be fine tomorrow.

Her assistant, Teddy, stuck his head in her office. "Mason wants to see you."

"I'll be right there."

Selah downed the rest of her coffee so the caffeine would get her through the day. She headed to his office.

The door was open, so she walked inside. Mason sat behind his desk, typing on his keyboard.

She cleared her throat.

He glanced up. "Why aren't you at Kieran's?"

Guess Kieran hadn't told Mason what happened. Typical. She always got left to do the dirty work. Still, her stomach clenched. "The project's almost finished. I had a call with his people earlier. We'll have one more on Monday, and it's done."

Mason studied her. "You didn't sleep last night."

She shrugged, not about to tell him she'd kissed one of his best friends.

"What's going on?" he pressed.

"I'm…" She might as well tell him because he would

find out eventually. "I quit."

"Quit?"

"I told Kieran I wouldn't be back and would finish up the project remotely."

Mason's forehead wrinkled. "What happened?"

She ground the toe of her shoe into the carpet. "It's personal."

"Tell me, so we don't have to waste time while I pull it out of you. You know I will."

He would. Selah breathed deeply, but that didn't calm her. Might as well get it over with. "We kissed. Kieran wants to date, but that's not possible."

"It's possible."

"I have rules."

"Ones you made up because some jerk broke your heart. It's not like Kieran is paying your salary."

"Semantics."

Mason raised a brow. "Or stubbornness."

She crossed her arms over her chest. "Not funny."

"No, because you're upset. Kieran must be, too."

Selah shrugged. That was his problem if he was.

"If I'd known about your dating rule, I would have never suggested you work on a project for him. I thought it would be a great way to get to know each other."

Selah tried to make sense of what Mason was saying. "Get to know each other?"

"He wanted to ask you out, and I thought you'd make a cute couple. So did Henry."

She stiffened. "You knew he was interested in me?"

Mason nodded.

Her jaw dropped. "That's why you wanted me to help Kieran with his project?"

Another nod.

She remembered how confused Kieran had been when she showed up at his office. "Was there a real project he needed help with?"

A sheepish expression crossed Mason's face. "Not at first, but your list told him to update the business suite, so it all worked out."

Her chest tightened. Heat burned behind her eyelids. "This is a game to you. Not only to you but to all your friends."

Mason's jaw tightened. "It's not a game, Selah."

"You used your position as my boss to pimp me out to your friend?"

He shook his head. "It wasn't like that. I was positive this would be good for you and Kieran."

"You came up with this…plan?" She wasn't sure what to call it.

"Me and Henry. We thought it was foolproof."

Unbelievable. She rubbed her arms, feeling dirty. "I put my job on hold and worked late to help your friend because you said it was important to you."

"I'm sorry. I thought this would work out." Mason stood. "I'll pay you extra."

"I don't want your money."

"What—"

"Stop." Her blood pressure spiraled. "I thought I was a

valuable part of TVT. But you treated me like a Reality TV contestant or one of those revolving door women you date."

"That's not true." He walked around his desk. "I got carried away after Kieran caught the garter at Adam's wedding. Henry kept teasing him about being the next to marry, and I want to win the bet."

Selah didn't understand what he meant. "Bet?"

Mason rubbed his neck. "Five years ago, my friends and I made a bet. Whoever is the last single man standing wins."

"What do you win?"

"As of two weeks ago, the pot had grown to nearly half a billion dollars. But it wasn't only the bet. Kieran wanted to ask you out on a date. Henry and I believed this would be better than going out for coffee or dinner."

"And more fun for all of you to watch."

Nodding, Mason lowered his gaze. "You haven't dated since Axel. I thought you might turn Kieran down, so I told him this would be the best way for you to be comfortable around him, so you'd say yes."

Her heart sank lower until it went splat at her feet. Metaphorically, but still.

She took a breath and another. "Except saying no or yes would be my choice. You took that away from me."

"I'll make it up to you. Name your price."

"I don't want your money." Selah could never spend all she'd made during the IPO and with her investments. "Helping Kieran was never about a bonus. I did it for you."

"Let me make this right." Mason sounded sincere, but…

"I'm taking time off." She needed a break, distance to

decide if TVT was where she wanted to be any longer. "I have personal time to use, and you don't need me here."

"I do. The launch—"

"You've managed with me at Kieran's. It'll be fine."

Mason shook his head. "I never meant for this to happen."

"This? You mean me finding out what you did and not liking it?" She waited for Mason to answer, but he didn't. "I've let you get away with stuff for years, so I understand why you thought you could again. You've never had consequences for your actions. This, however, was more like a schoolboy's prank."

He appeared embarrassed, but she wouldn't be swayed. "When will you be back?"

She straightened. Her insides trembled, but no way would she show it. "I'm not sure if I'll return."

His mouth gaped. "But—"

"I've done everything in my power to help you and make TVT a success. I'm proud of my efforts and what we've accomplished. You've said I'm your right-hand person, yet you treated me like a pawn in some silly game. I deserve better."

"You do, but Kieran—"

"The fact he went along with this tells me he's someone I'd never want to date."

"Selah, please." Mason's voice cracked. "Take all the time you need, but don't quit. I need you."

Once upon a time, she might have believed him but no longer. "Goodbye, Mason."

Chapter Eight

Sunday at Dash's house, the usual crowd showed up and headed to the courtyard in the back. A large charcuterie board was on the table full of donuts, French toast sticks, mini egg casseroles, fruit, cheese, scones, pastries, and bacon kabobs. Iris had outdone herself again.

If only Kieran had an appetite.

He glanced at his friends seated around the large table. Opposite him, Henry sat in the middle, telling one of his stories and basking in the attention from Wes and Mason. Blaise and Brett listened, albeit seemingly half-heartedly, while exchanging last week's gains in the stock market. Adam, looking tan and rested after his honeymoon, stared at his phone with a goofy grin on his face. Cambria must have texted him. As Dash grabbed a donut, Iris brought out another round of mimosas.

A typical brunch.

Except Kieran wasn't in the mood for company or food. Food no longer appealed to him. He'd barely slept since Friday. Not even work held his attention for more than a minute or two. Nothing mattered, except…

Iris set a mimosa in front of him before refilling his coffee cup. "You okay?"

"I…" He had no idea what to say, so he drank half the champagne and orange juice mixture.

"Everything will work out." Henry's not-a-care-in-the-world tone grated on Kieran's nerves.

Mason hung his head. "I'm not sure it will."

"Have you heard from Selah, Mase?" Kieran asked.

"Not a word," Mason admitted. "I've tried to reach her since Friday. My calls go straight to voice mail. You?"

"Nothing. She probably blocked me." Kieran didn't blame her.

"I don't know what to do," Mason groaned. "Her assistant helped Selah pack her belongings on Friday. He cried in her office for an hour after she left. He doesn't think she's coming back. I don't, either."

Blaise held a coffee cup. "Has Selah officially resigned?"

"No. She said she needed time." Mason used his fork to push around pieces of raspberry blintzes. He looked haggard. "But I've never seen her this angry."

"Any idea if she's still in town?" Adam asked.

Mason shrugged. "She might have gone to visit her parents—"

"She wouldn't go to see them," Kieran interrupted.

Mason glared at him. "How would you know?"

"She told me they don't approve of her working for TVT." Kieran didn't want to play the "Who Knows Selah Best" game, but Mason could be clueless at times. "They didn't want Selah to drop out of grad school. If they heard what happened, it would prove them right."

Mason slumped in his chair. "She never mentioned there was a problem with them."

"Did you ever ask?"

A sheepish expression formed on Mason's face. "I should have. I should have done a lot of things."

Dash shrugged. "She's only one employee. No one is irreplaceable."

"You don't know Selah." Kieran took a sip.

Mason nodded. "Everyone says I'm TVT. The vision and the heart, yes, but she's the brain behind it. She's the reason all the parts function together, including me."

"How did this even happen?" Blaise asked.

"Kieran caught Cambria's garter. He wanted someone to catch his kiss. Selah seemed a perfect choice, but we messed up." Henry sounded contrite.

Not trusting his voice, Kieran nodded.

"We all messed up," Henry continued. "But if you have feelings for Selah, don't let her get away without a fight."

"Good luck with that." Mason scrubbed his face. "I apologized, but she didn't care."

"Would you?" Wes asked, accusation in his tone.

"Yes." The word shot out of Mason's mouth.

"No," Kieran said a beat later. "It was a game to us."

Mason shook his head. "The means justify the end."

"Not if you're dishonest," Wes countered.

Adam nodded. "Deception and games will only blow up in your face."

Brett lowered his coffee cup. "Kieran was in a position of power."

"I wasn't her real boss," Kieran countered.

"No, but Mason was." Brett pointed out. "He took advantage of that. Of Selah."

Mason's lower lip stuck out. "And so did you by going along with our plan."

"As if you left me a choice." Kieran wasn't blameless. He hadn't told her the truth. "I should have asked her out to dinner instead of trusting Mason and Henry."

It was Henry's turn to nod. "We should have stayed out of it."

"I thought this was foolproof." Mason raised his glass. "I mean, it's working for me."

Kieran's lips parted. "What do you mean?"

"Nothing." Mason sipped his mimosa.

Blaise set his coffee on the table and picked up his mimosa. "Must be something in the water."

Brett leaned forward. "Please tell us you're not pulling the same thing with somebody else."

"I'm…" Mason stared into his drink. "It's different."

"Dude…" Dash shook his head. "Even I know better than this."

Blaise laughed before taking a sip of his drink.

Kieran studied Mason. "So that's where you came up with this idea?"

Mason shrugged. "It seemed like a good idea at the time. Henry agreed."

Wes grimaced. "Henry thought it was a good idea to fill

his ice bucket at the Plaza naked and got locked out of his room. I wouldn't use him as a reference for having good judgment."

A wicked grin lit up Henry's face. "Wes has a point. Though I met a lovely woman who was happy to…help me that evening."

Kieran had heard that story too many times. Part of him believed it to be one more of Henry's tall tales. "Come clean, Mason. I didn't tell Selah the truth and lost my chance. Don't be an idiot. I don't want you or anyone at this table ever to feel the way I do right now."

"You can't give up," Adam said.

Kieran wasn't a quitter, but… "I don't want to, but if she won't answer my calls or text…"

"Stupid tech guys. Put down the phone and stop looking at your screen." Brett's intense gaze pinned Kieran. "Go to her. Talk to her face-to-face. Ask her to let you start over."

"Start over," Kieran repeated.

Brett nodded. "Apologize and ask her out the way you intended before Henry and Mason got involved. If she says no, you walk away."

"I don't want to walk away."

"Then convince her to give you a second chance."

"If you need any help," Henry offered.

"No!" everyone at the table shouted in unison. Well, everyone except Mason.

They all laughed.

"Guess I have nothing to lose," Kieran admitted.

"Nope," Adam said. "But you have everything to gain."

Adam and Brett shared a knowing glance. Leave it to the two married guys to tell Kieran what he needed to hear.

He hoped Selah gave him a second chance. Only he didn't want her to catch his kiss. This time, he wanted her to catch his heart.

* * *

As another episode of The Great British Bake Off played on Sunday afternoon, Selah folded her last load of laundry. Her holey leggings and stained T-shirt didn't look like anything a person would wear if they had another choice, but this weekend was about making herself comfortable. That was why she'd taken clean towels from her linen closet and washed them to give her more to do.

Pathetic.

Yes, but she needed to keep occupied now that her condo was hospital-operating-room spotless. Not a speck of dust remained, and the wood floors gleamed. Not one item was out of place. Okay, stuff rarely was, but she'd gone through everything, tossing or donating things to the animal rescue's thrift store. She'd reorganized every closet, drawer, and cabinet.

It had only taken two days.

Okay, she was usually organized and tidy, but she thought it would take her longer. At least a week. Now she would have nothing to do tomorrow.

Monday.

"What do I want to do next?"

Selah rarely missed a day of work unless she was sick. Her unused vacation days accrued. The mornings she'd spent at Kieran's had been an anomaly—and a mistake. Heading to the office or working from home on the weekends had become as familiar to her as breathing. From day one, she'd thrown herself into TVT and pushed herself to exhaustion more times than she wanted to count. All for Mason. Yes, she had a ton of money, but wealth hadn't been the driving force. She'd enjoyed contributing, feeling as if she'd made a difference, and the sense of belonging.

But she'd also liked the respect. At least, Selah thought she'd been respected. Some of her coworkers still did, but actions spoke louder than words, which told her Mason didn't respect her. He and Kieran had treated her as a bad punchline in an unfunny joke.

For the first time in forever, she didn't want to be at TVT.

Not on a Sunday or during the week.

And that was…telling.

"What do I want?"

She glanced at the TV. The dessert looked delicious, but baking didn't interest her.

Ideas streamed in her mind. She had a bucket list of places she wanted to visit, charities to research, and states to go to that didn't have income tax if she ever moved. She wasn't a billionaire, but being a multi-millionaire gave her endless possibilities.

What do I…

The answer hit hard and fast.

She blew out a breath. "I want…more."

Not money or accolades or anything material. Selah wanted community beyond the office, companionship with more than the coworkers who shared common interests, and…love.

The pounding of her heart intensified as if to drive home that point. Or perhaps thinking about love heightened her awareness. Either way…

She glanced around her condo that she'd called home for the past four years. It was lovely and comfortable and insanely expensive, but it lacked warmth. A pet or two might help. So would a boyfriend, but…

"I won't find what I want without making some changes."

It was as simple—or complicated, if she wanted to be honest with herself—as that.

What had happened with Kieran and Mason made her view everything in a new light. She enjoyed working. Doing stuff for others lit her up, too. But it was no longer enough.

Selah opened her laptop, created a document, and typed a resignation letter.

A knock sounded.

That was odd, considering this was a secure building. Unless it was Mrs. Karis, who lived across the hall.

Selah padded over the rug in her bare feet and opened the door.

Kieran stood there with the tips of his fingers tucked into his shorts pockets. Dressed so casually with messy hair and stubble, he shouldn't look as good as he did after how he'd treated her. "Hey."

She clutched the knob. "Did Mason tell you where I lived?"

"No, Dash Cabot."

That made no sense. "How did he know?"

"The guy's a genius. He has ways." Kieran glanced to the right and left. He removed his fingers from his pockets and placed his arms at his sides. "Can I come in, please?"

"No." She clutched the knob.

"For a few minutes, please," he added. "I'd rather not have this conversation in the hallway."

This building was quiet, but he had a point. She let him inside and closed the door behind him. "Make it fast."

"Busy?"

She lifted her chin. "I'm writing my resignation letter."

Kieran's face paled. He took a breath. "I'm sorry for what happened. It was never a game to me. I never set out to hurt you. I only wanted to go out with you and planned on doing that until my friends got involved. I knew better, but I trusted them, and I lost… I lost everything."

"Everything?"

His gaze met hers. "You."

He sounded sincere. But so had Axel. A little more distance between them would be good. She stepped away from Kieran. "I'm not sure what you want me to say."

"I'd like a second chance."

"Why?"

"I want to try this my way." He wiped his hands on his shorts and stuck out his right hand. "I'm Kieran O'Neal."

"What are you doing?"

"Starting over if you're willing."

Selah wasn't sure of anything except she hadn't forgotten their kiss. And he was what made her rethink what she wanted.

Worth the risk?

Maybe. But that was good enough for now.

She shook his hand. "I'm Selah Burton."

He held her hand longer than it was socially acceptable before letting go. "Would you like to go out with me?"

Selah hesitated. "When?"

"Now."

"I…"

"We need at least one date before we talk about a wedding date."

Her mouth gaped. "Wait a minute. We just met and only kissed once."

His eyes twinkled. "We can remedy that."

"I'm not interested in playing games."

"I'm not playing."

She stared at him. His gaze was dark and locked on her. "You're serious."

"I am." Kieran didn't miss a beat. "When you know, you know, and I do."

"This isn't what I expected to happen."

"Me, either, but sometimes, you have to go with it."

"Did Dash say that, too?"

"No, Henry." Kieran smiled at her. "I fell for you the moment you walked into Mason's office. Let's go and eat.

We can get to know each other better."

"I'm not sure what to say."

"I'm laying it all out there. Please give me a chance to show you how perfect we'll be together."

Her heart shifted. Affection—it had to be that and not love, right—overflowed. "I'm not used to trusting myself after what happened before. I want to believe you."

"All you have to do is try."

"I can try. But if I ever fell in love again, it would be with a guy like you."

"That's good enough for now." He came closer and kissed her on the lips.

It might still be July, but the fourth was long past. That didn't stop the fireworks from exploding inside her.

Kieran backed away. "Okay?"

Maybe he was onto something. Her heart pounded. "We need to try that again, and then we can go out."

"Sounds like a plan." He pressed his mouth against hers once again.

* * *

Each day for the past week, a bouquet arrived at Selah's apartment. The colorful blossoms made the place feel more like a flower shop than a home, but the fragrance wafting through the place was divine. This Saturday morning was no different. She placed the newest arrangement—lilies this time—on the dresser in her bedroom.

The funny thing was they weren't from Kieran. Oh, he'd

bought her gifts—a stuffed animal, a coffee collection, and chocolates—since they started dating on Sunday, but the flowers were from Mason. He didn't want to accept her resignation letter and was trying to change her mind.

Selah, however, was enjoying this time off. She'd been able to see Kieran every day. They'd had coffee, lunch, and four dinners. On the days he hadn't much time, he'd still stopped by for a few minutes. The effort—and the kisses—told her they had something special. And he was doing everything in his power to make up for what he'd done.

As for her not working…

Sleeping in, catching up on her reading, and doing things she'd put off for far too long was fun. She no longer needed coffee to get through the day, but she could enjoy a cup.

Mason might want her back, but she was in no rush to return to TVT. She wasn't ready to retire, but whatever she ended up doing—working at TVT or a new place—changes had to happen. She wanted to have a life, especially now that Kieran was part of it.

A knock sounded.

Her heart leaped. She hurried to the door and opened it.

Kieran stood in shorts and a polo shirt. He held boxes of food and a paper bag. "Brunch has arrived."

"And here I thought it was only my boyfriend." She kissed him on the lips. "But whatever you brought smells delicious."

"It's the chef's choice and coffee cake. Oh, and coffee."

Had it only been two weeks ago that they'd met there?

It seemed like another lifetime, given all that had happened.

She motioned him inside and closed the door. "Let's eat before my stomach starts growling."

They sat next to each other at her table and ate. Kieran kept staring at her.

That was weird. "What?"

"I was thinking of our first brunch together."

"That was nice, but I prefer this."

"Me, too." He took a sip of coffee. "Even the food tastes better."

"It does." Selah didn't know if that was because of a new chef or being in a relationship with Kieran. Whichever it was, she would take it.

"Don't forget the coffee cake."

She noticed the one box they'd forgotten to open. "Oops. How did we forget that?"

He shrugged with a big grin on his face. "Nothing wrong with saving the best for last. I remembered how much you like it."

"I do." She reached across the table, grabbed the box, and set it between them before lifting the lid. Something sparkled on top of the coffee cake. It sat on a small circle of parchment paper.

Wait. What?

Selah took a closer look.

A...diamond ring.

The air whooshed from her lungs. She glanced at Kieran. "I have no idea what to say."

He plucked the ring off the coffee cake and dropped to one knee. "The first time I mentioned marriage was only a week ago, but I was serious. Spending time with you since then just reaffirmed how I feel. I want to wake up next to you every morning and go to bed with you each night. I can't imagine my life without you in it. Selah, I love you. will you marry me?"

She struggled to breathe. This was unbelievable, but it felt so right—oh-so-right—even if it was lightning fast and not how she usually operated. Her heart, however, knew. And that was enough for her.

"I love you, too." Tears of joy filled her eyes. "And yes, I'll marry you."

Kieran slid the ring onto her finger and kissed her.

The enormous diamond, surrounded by smaller ones, shot colorful prisms of light around the apartment. Selah stared at it. "The ring is beautiful."

"Not as beautiful as you." He kissed her again. "Let's finish eating because we only have a few hours before we meet with Rachael Saunders."

"Who?"

"She's the event planner who did my friend Adam's wedding earlier in July. Mason suggested we talk to her."

"Mason knew you were proposing."

Kieran nodded. "He gave the thumbs up on the ring."

"This is all happening so fast."

His forehead creased. "Too fast?"

Selah thought for a moment. "No."

"Good, because I want a short engagement, so pull out your calendar."

It was the beginning of August. "How short?"

"I'm thinking two or three…"

"Months?"

"Weeks."

Her heart slammed against her rib cage. Something that happened a lot around him. Selah had to remember that billionaires did things differently. She smiled at him. "Sounds great to me."

Epilogue

August

Underneath a large white tent strung with tulle, lights, and flowers, Mason stood with his friends, watching Selah and Kieran dance to a song played by two pianists and a drummer. The newlyweds stared into each other's eyes, and wide smiles lit up their faces. It was as if they were dancing alone without a hundred of their closest family members and friends watching them.

Mason was happy for the couple, but he would rather be anywhere else at the moment. Unfortunately, leaving wasn't an option. Getting blackout drunk probably wasn't a good idea, either, though it had crossed his mind twice already.

Henry handed him a glass of champagne. "This is becoming a habit. One of you tech guys as the groom. Rachael Saunders as the wedding planner."

Mason took a sip, forcing himself not to chug. "Only four of us left."

Three for him to win the bet. That should make him

happier than it did.

He drank more champagne.

"I never imagined hosting a wedding at my house, but Rachael did a lovely job." Henry tilted his head toward the other side of the tent, which was where Mason had seen her last. "She's been working nonstop for the past week. I let her stay in the guest house so she wouldn't have to commute to her apartment."

"It was nice of you to offer Kieran and Selah your backyard." However, the word didn't begin to describe Henry's elegant estate.

He shrugged. "I owed them, and they didn't leave Rachael much time to plan their nuptials."

"Must be why people have longer engagements."

"Is that what you plan to do?" Curiosity laced each word.

He focused on Henry, not wanting to be…distracted by someone else. "Let's see what Blaise, Dash, and Wes do first."

Henry rolled his eyes. "Still intent on winning the bet."

"I started it."

"You can afford to lose."

Mason could, except… "I'm not dating anyone."

Not for his lack of trying.

Though he hadn't tried. Not really. And now he was alone and she…

He shook the thought from his head before taking another drink.

"You could be," Henry urged.

Mason shrugged. The less he said, the better. His friend

didn't need to know he'd had his chance and blown it. Big time. Only he wouldn't be able to recover the way Kieran had. "I'm happy how I am."

Liar.

He looked around to see who said that, but a glance showed Mason it must have been inside his head.

Great.

Now he was talking to himself.

Henry studied him. "You have more than most, but you seemed happier at Adam's wedding."

Another shrug, even though what Henry said was true. If Mason could go back to that night, he would…

What was he thinking?

Nothing would be different.

He would have only messed up in some other spectacular way. "I'm fine."

"No, you're not." Henry eyed Mason warily. "Selah is your right-hand person at work. Are you upset she's marrying Kieran?"

"No." Without her, his company would have never succeeded the way it had. He relied on her more than anyone else. And they'd worked out an agreement. If he allowed her to work fewer hours and never play any games with her, she'd promised not to quit. "They fit. It's time she found someone who treats her well, and Kieran does. Though if he hurts her, he'll regret the day he was born."

Henry laughed. "Did you tell Kieran that?"

"Selah did. She knows I have her back."

"Who has yours?"

"You and the others." Except Mason had told no one what had been going on in his personal life. Not even Selah knew.

"Rachael is lovely and single. I can't see her with master Dashiell, but perhaps Wes or Blaise."

Mason gripped his glass. He forced himself to drink.

"If you want to meet a woman, I'll arrange it. Hadley Lowell is a matchmaker in San Francisco. She'll find you a wife." Henry glanced at the crowd. "Brett and Laurel. Adam and Cambria. Kieran and Selah. I can't wait to introduce the next billionaire of Silicon Forest to his bride."

"What do you get out of doing that?"

"More godchildren."

The guy was unbelievable. Mason's hand flew up, palm facing Henry. "No matchmaking. I had as much or more to do with Kieran and Selah getting together than you."

Henry waved his hand as if brushing away a fly. Only there weren't any insects in his backyard. Bugs didn't adhere to no-fly zones, so Henry's staff must have done something to control them. "It was still my idea."

"One that wouldn't have happened without me. And we almost ruined Kieran's chance with her."

Kieran was right that simply asking out Selah would have been less complicated. Would a more straightforward approach work for Mason and…?

He would never know.

"It's time for the bridal toss," one of the piano players said into his microphone. "Can all the single ladies come onto the dance floor, please?"

Rachael handed a bouquet to the bride and positioned her between the two pianos. Kieran stared at his bride with such love it made Mason's mouth go dry.

Henry snagged the glass out of Mason's hands. "Looks like I won't be able to catch the garter tonight."

"How long do you think being a two-fisted champagne drinker will work?"

"Until all of you are married, so four more weddings."

Blaise, Dash, and Wes joined them.

Wes rubbed his neck. "It's almost that time again."

"I'm telling you." Blaise shook his head. "There's something in the water."

"Does anyone want to volunteer as tribute?" Dash asked.

Everyone laughed.

"It might not come close to one of us." Mason glanced at Kieran, removing the garter from his bride's leg while a flirty tune played.

Blaise motioned to Henry. "Why don't we grab champagne glasses like our friend here so we can't catch it?"

Henry beamed. "I knew my brilliance would be contagious."

"Same rules as at Adam's wedding." Brett came up. "Don't ruin Selah and Kieran's big day if the garter comes your way. Catch it."

As Selah turned away from the crowd, women jockeyed for position.

"On three," the pianist said. "One, two, three…"

A red-headed woman caught the flowers and held both hands overhead as if she'd scored a touchdown.

"Now, it's the gentlemen's time," the other piano player said. "All single men out on the dance floor."

"That's your cue." Brett motioned them out there.

Blaise scowled. "You're such a dad now."

Brett smirked. "Wait until Noelle is old enough to play soccer, and I have a coach's whistle. I'll blow it to keep you guys in line."

Henry stood on the edge of the dance floor, but he had no free hands. The guy might be onto something.

With a wide smile, Kieran looked at each of them before facing away.

"On three," the second pianist said. "One, two, three…"

The wisp of lace and silk flew directly at Wes until its path curved and landed against Mason's chest.

His friends cheered.

Henry raised both flutes in the air. "Looks like we know who the next groom will be. I wonder what kind of wedding Rachael will plan for you and your bride."

As Kieran gave Mason a thumbs up, Selah laughed before shaking her head. Rachael met his gaze for a nanosecond. An idea formed in his head. More risky than brilliant, but what did he have to lose at this point? "Let's hope she wants to plan a wedding at a winery."

Blaise gasped.

Wes's forehead creased.

"Wait, what?" Dash asked.

Adam and Brett laughed.

Henry grinned. "Oh, this sounds like fun."

Either fun or an epic failure. Only time would tell Mason which it would be.

But first, he needed to ask Kieran the best way to apologize.

The Game Changer

MELISSA McCLONE

Chapter One

July

With stone walls and floors, large windows, and an arched wood ceiling strung with lights, Mount Hood's Silcox Hut was an excellent venue for the intimate wedding, especially since Mason Reese wasn't the billionaire getting married.

A grin spread across his face.

Now, all he needed was for four more weddings to occur.

The sooner, the better.

So he would be the winner.

In every sense of the word.

As a popular dance tune played, people laughed and drank. A few danced in a small area.

Not him.

Dancing wasn't his thing.

Now champagne…

Mason grabbed a filled flute from the bar. He didn't have

to drive—Timberline Lodge provided SUVs to transport people to and from the wedding—so he could indulge in as many drinks as he wanted. Blaise Mortenson required security after a run-in with a reporter, so Mason could have grabbed a ride with him, too. Or he could have accepted invitations to stay at either Henry Davenport's or Wes Lockhart's lodges, which were a short drive away in Hood Hamlet. Both had drivers who doubled as bodyguards.

Mason enjoyed staying with his friends, but after spending three days at a tech retreat—a misnomer since it was more like a conference but with fewer attendees—he wanted a night by himself. That way, he could sleep in before tomorrow's farewell wedding brunch, which was being held at the lodge. A few extra minutes of shuteye might not make a huge difference, but he didn't want to start the week more exhausted than usual.

Cambria and Adam Zeile kissed for the hundredth time that day. If Adam weren't such a good friend and Cambria perfect for said friend, Mason would find their PDA sickly sweet. But their love and affection for each other were palpable. A bit surprising given how short a time they'd known each other. They'd raced to the altar weeks after meeting because they saw no reason to wait. Though *sprint* might be a better word. Still, he was thrilled for the happy couple and, most especially, himself. Today's wedding brought Mason one step closer to winning the bet.

One down.

Four to go.

That refrain had been playing in his head ever since

hearing the bride and groom say, "I do."

He sipped his champagne. The bubbly went down smoothly.

Of course, Adam would splurge on the good stuff for his nuptials. Everything tonight was top-of-the-line. Again, not surprising, but the wedding would set the standard for those that followed. Well, when the next four of their friends married.

Mason wasn't getting married. At least not until after Blaise, Dash, Kieran, and Wes.

Perhaps not even after them.

Mason needed to win the bet—his bet—before he considered a serious relationship of any kind.

Five years ago, he'd dreamed up the last single-man-standing wager. It had begun as a joke when Henry Davenport teased his friends for being tech geeks and not having girlfriends. Surprisingly, the other Billionaires of Silicon Forest—what the media and folks around town called the six of them—expressed interest in a bet. Since all were single and not looking to get married, why not put money on it? Given their friendly competitive spirits, a wager not only made sense but would also be fun.

Mason came up with the bet, and it was on. They each put in ten million dollars—the stakes needed to be high to count. Now, the original sixty million had grown to hundreds of millions thanks to Blaise Mortenson's investment algorithm.

All Mason had to do was outlast the other five. Well, four, now that Adam was married.

No problem.

Mason had little time to date and zero interest in getting serious with a woman. His company required his full attention, so he knew he would win eventually. He hadn't thought the others would be so slow to fall in love and figured the bet would last two or three years tops. But nope. It had been five years. Oh, Mason enjoyed dating and did, but he kept things casual. With so many wonderful women in this world, why limit himself to only one?

But he was happy for Adam.

As the couple posed for a photograph, Mason raised his champagne flute in a proper toast.

To Cambria. Thanks to you, I'm one step closer to winning the bet.

Mason took a sip.

"Why aren't you dancing with one of the lovely ladies?" Henry asked.

Most were dancing as a group, but that answer wouldn't sway his friend. Mason stared over the lip of his glass. "I'm enjoying the view from here."

"Looking will only get you so far. Now touching…" Henry wagged his eyebrows.

Mason laughed. The guy had a higher net worth than any of them, but Henry had never worked a day in his life. He'd had a trust fund growing up and inherited more from his parents. His life was one of excess, revolving around partying, dressing so people noticed him, giving away his money, and spending time with his young goddaughter, Noelle.

"Then why aren't *you* dancing?" Mason asked.

"Weddings put people in romantic frames of mind. I don't want to give a woman the false hope that I'm the one, and the only one, for her."

That was thoughtful of Henry, except… "If she knows of your reputation, that won't happen."

Henry shrugged. "I'd rather not take any chances. The fewer hearts I break, the better."

That was one way to look at it. Avoiding conflict and confrontation was another. Henry was a romantic at heart, even if he denied it. He enjoyed playing matchmaker and taking credit when his friends fell in love. He claimed to be the one who brought Adam and Cambria together, but Mother Nature's torrential rain that caused a mudslide was the reason, not Henry.

"The night's still young." Henry surveyed the room. "Let's meet in the Ram's Head Bar at the Lodge when this soiree ends."

"I'm in." Mason would enjoy a nightcap with his friends. "I'll post about it on the group chat to make sure everyone knows."

The group chat app *his* company developed.

Pride made him stand taller.

Kieran O'Neal, who'd caught the bridal garter and wore it around his arm, danced with a trio of pretty women. He was all smiles, enjoying himself. Maybe secretly, Kieran wanted to settle down, and catching the garter was the push he needed. That would be awesome, if true. It would mean one less single billionaire to compete for the prize.

"Sounds good." Henry glanced over at Brett and Laurel Matthews. "Unfortunately, Brett's out."

"I assumed he was." Brett was out of most things they did these days. He managed billions with his investment company and was on his way to being a billionaire himself. The son of the Davenports' housekeeper—he'd grown up with Henry—Brett was a good guy and the only one who had a kid. The guy showed up to things when he could, especially football Sundays, but ever since his daughter, Noelle, had been born on Christmas Day over a year and a half ago, that wasn't often.

As Mason sipped from his glass, a flash of honey caught his attention. The color, not the sticky stuff bees made and bears loved. He squinted for a better look.

A single honey-colored hair plait had been artfully braided and belonged to a woman speaking to the bride and groom. Her light-blue skirt and matching jacket showed off some curves, but he wanted to see her face.

He waited for her to turn, but she didn't.

"Who are you looking at?" Henry asked.

"No one." Mason didn't want Henry to play matchmaker. "I've heard of brides being radiant, but Adam is practically glowing."

"The glowing groom." Henry grinned. "I like that."

"You can take credit for it."

"I believe I will. Thanks."

Mason kept his gaze on the woman with the newlyweds. She still faced away from him. He didn't know why she intrigued him so much, but if anyone knew her, Henry would. "Do you know the person talking to Adam and Cambria."

Henry glanced around until his gaze zeroed in on his target. "Oh, that's Rachael Saunders."

Rachael Saunders. The name wasn't familiar to Mason. "Is she a friend of Cambria's?"

Henry rolled his eyes. "I shouldn't be surprised you don't know of her. You don't throw many parties."

Huh? What did that have to do with Rachael? "You lost me."

"Rachael is a rising event coordinator in Portland. She's becoming the go-to person for the younger movers and shakers in town, and her client base is expanding into the baby boomers, too. She's known as the posh planner."

Mason had little need for event planners. If his company put on an event, someone else organized it. If he invited people to his home, he hired Dash Cabot's housekeeper, Iris, to oversee things. But posh described Rachael's outfit. It appeared to be a mix of retro and modern styles, but Mason wouldn't know how vintage it was until he saw the front. His right-hand employee, Selah Burton, had educated him in non-tech things like fashion and pop culture. She claimed he needed to discuss more than video games and blockbuster movie franchises with people, namely the board of directors, who expected their founder and CEO to be adept at adulting in front of stockholders who showed up for the annual meeting.

As a server walked past the newlyweds and planner, the woman—Rachael—turned, giving Mason a complete view of her face.

Whoa.

He staggered as if shoved in the chest, and whatever hit him radiated out from the spot.

Henry touched Mason's shoulder. "Are you okay?"

No. But he didn't dare tell Henry that.

Mason struggled to catch his breath. His pulse pounded.

What just happened?

Not trusting his voice, Mason nodded. He forced his attention off the woman's pretty face.

Henry laughed. "Too much bubbly."

Mason nodded a second time. He'd drunk two glasses earlier, so that and his tiredness explained his reaction. Still, he glanced at the woman one more time. She'd turned away. Probably a good thing. He wasn't used to being so attracted to anyone and didn't like having his attention captured that way.

"Why did you ask about Rachael?" Henry asked.

"I didn't recognize her." Which was one hundred percent the truth. "I was curious."

Henry rubbed his chin. "Curious?"

"Yes, since I know or have met most of the people here. Given she's working the event, it makes sense why no one introduced us."

"Yes, it does." Henry's gaze bounced from Mason to her. "Adam and Cambria have nothing but nice things to say about her. I found her friendly and eloquent. Plus, she's lovely. Few women her age could pull off that outfit with pearls."

Mine. Mason wanted to growl.

What is wrong with me?

A wedding planner would have marriage on the brain if she weren't married already. Someone like that—her—wasn't for him. Perhaps in five or ten years after he'd won the bet and had his company running the way he wanted it, but now wasn't the time to fall for anyone.

No matter how beautiful she might be.

"I wouldn't know." He loosened his grip on the flute before he snapped the stem in half. "You're the one who's into fashion accessories."

Mason downed the remaining champagne and fought the urge to grimace.

Laughter lit Henry's eyes. "The bartender will pour you shots if you're so inclined."

Mason raised his chin. "Champagne shots are the new thing."

"Champagne Jell-O shots, perhaps." Henry's forehead wrinkled. "I'm all about excess, but there are much better ways to enjoy a thousand-dollar bottle of bubbly."

"You're right." Okay, Henry hadn't noticed Mason's reaction to Rachael. Unless he hadn't had one—that big of one, at least—and the attraction was all in his head. Perhaps being at a wedding was messing with his mind, as Henry mentioned. "I'll have my glass refilled and sip the civilized way."

"I'll accompany you to the bar. On our way there, I'll introduce you to Rachael."

Mason's stomach dropped. He might be overreacting to his initial impression of her, but meeting the event planner didn't seem like a smart idea. "Why would you do that?"

Mischief gleamed in Henry's eyes. "Are you serious?"

Yes, except saying that might raise his friend's suspicions. Mason shrugged.

"Mase, Mase, Mase. When do we ever need a reason to speak with a beautiful woman?" Henry's long exhale was typical when he lost his patience with his friends. "You've made billions by making it easier for people to communicate on their phones, tablets, and computers, yet you're no better than our young Dashiell when it comes to talking with the opposite sex."

Dash was the youngest of their friend group and nicknamed Wonderkid. He was the smartest in the room—it didn't matter which room or who was in it, which was saying something since they were all tech guys. Well, not Henry, but he'd graduated from Harvard or one of those Ivies on the East Coast. Dash didn't have the best social skills when dealing with women or his friends. Sometimes, his words didn't appear to keep up with his mind.

But Mason wasn't like that. "Stop right there."

Once a person looked beyond Dash's words, they saw a good person with a generous heart. But Mason's interpersonal skills were light years ahead of the guy's.

"I might not have social skills like you and Wes, well, old Wes, have." Wes Lockhart was another of their group. He'd been fighting cancer but was finally in remission. Wes, however, wasn't the same as before his illness. "But I'm nothing like Dash," Mason added. "Trust me."

"You're protesting a bit too much." Henry sounded

amused. "Prove it."

"By?"

Henry tilted his chin toward the event planner.

As Mason stared at her, warmth flowed through him. It must be the champagne shot—or the entire glass and other drinks before that one. Okay, maybe not.

No problem.

So what if he felt a lightning bolt of…something when he saw her face? No big deal. He'd met plenty of beautiful women—from supermodels to actresses. This was nothing.

Still, he hesitated.

"Come on," Henry urged. "It's not like meeting her will change your life."

Of course, not. She wasn't for Mason. No woman was.

He swallowed around the lump in his throat.

"True." Meeting her would prove he'd felt nothing. He would move on and forget her. "Let's get this over with. I want another drink."

Chapter Two

Rachael reviewed the rest of the reception schedule with the newlyweds. She hadn't sat in hours, but making certain events happened without a hitch meant being on her feet, ready to do whatever needed to be done. Investing in a pair of stylish yet comfortable shoes had been her smartest start-up purchase. "If there's anyone you want to speak with, now's the time."

"We've talked to everyone at least once, so we're good." Cambria glowed. She was the quintessential bride in her sleeveless white lace gown. "This isn't a big space, but you were right. It's the absolute perfect spot for our wedding."

A thrill shot through Rachael. "I'm happy you feel that way."

She'd had a feeling Silcox Hut's rustic and romantic atmosphere would appeal to the couple. The place fitted their criteria perfectly. It was on Mount Hood—they'd met only a few miles from here—private and would accommodate them and thirty guests. The venue usually booked up to a year or two in advance, but a rare cancellation had made tonight possible. The Silcox Hut's staff had their wedding routine dialed in, and everything had gone as planned, but Adam hadn't wanted Cambria to worry about anything on their wedding day, so he'd hired Rachael. Other than those employed there, she'd been the first to arrive, and she would be the last to leave. The florists would pick up their items at a pre-arranged time tomorrow morning.

But she needed to check off one last thing before the bride and groom left. Well, headed down the mountain a mile for their wedding night in a fireplace room at the Timberline Lodge. Tomorrow afternoon, they would go on a ten-day honeymoon—the destination unknown to all but the groom.

"I have one final question." The two photographers had stayed busy tonight, but Rachael wanted to make sure nothing was missed. She did this at all her events, but this wedding introduced her and her company, The Posh Planner, to a different clientele level—billionaires—so she was extra careful. More business from that crowd would up-level her business. "Are there any other photographs you want to be taken?"

As the bride and groom talked between themselves, they recalled several poses taken so far.

Rachael stayed quiet. Only they knew if they needed more, but watching the couple filled her with longing. The love these two shared made her want the same thing. Rachael's heart agreed. It wasn't as if she hadn't tried to meet guys, but no matter how many times she swiped right or dated, romance eluded her. The men she'd gone out with didn't like her working weekends, which made things difficult because that was part of her job.

Not only a job, though.

Event planning was her passion.

Her life.

Through it, she'd found a way to climb back after her father's gambling habit left them penniless and a laughingstock to former friends. She wasn't at the top yet, but she would be with more events like this one. Of that, she knew.

Sure, falling in love like Cambria and Adam would be nice—okay, great—but her business was growing each month thanks to word of mouth from her clients. This wasn't the time to slow down or get distracted. A relationship would have to wait.

"The list you gave the photographers had more suggestions than we'd come up with on our own." Cambria glanced up at her husband with heart-eyes. "I think we have enough."

Adam ran his finger along his wife's jawline. "I'll never have enough pictures of you."

As a blush stole up Cambria's neck to her cheeks, she sighed.

Her husband kissed the top of her head. "All we're missing are the shots as we leave."

Cambria nodded, but her attention remained focused on Adam. The way it had been since the ceremony began.

"Then we're all set." Someday, Rachael would find a love like that. One that was unconditional. Her career or her family wouldn't matter. Only a deep, abiding love would. "I just wanted to make sure."

"Thanks. Our wedding day has been a dream come true." Cambria laced her fingers with Adam's. "I appreciate having you here to help us."

"You've gone above and beyond," Adam agreed.

"Thank you." Rachael's entire body felt as if it were smiling. "I've enjoyed every minute. I'm so glad I could be a part of your special day."

Cambria shimmied her shoulders. "Us, too."

"The three of you have set a high bar for the next wedding." Henry Davenport, who Rachael had met earlier, joined them. He was a billionaire but not one of the Billionaires of Silicon Forest. Those were the six tech guys—Adam was one—who'd founded companies in and around the Portland Metro Area.

Henry motioned to a man with dark brown hair and brown eyes with gold flecks. Rachael noticed him earlier, but they hadn't met. He'd ditched his bowtie and unbuttoned the top of his dress shirt, but that only made him more attractive.

"Rachael Sanders, this is Mason Reese," Henry said. "The two of you should talk. Every billionaire needs an event planner like you in his contacts. Do you have a card for him?"

"I do." She pulled one from her skirt pocket. Mason was handsome like all the rest of the groom's friends. Rachael didn't know if he was one of the tech guys, but a billionaire was a billionaire. She hoped one or more hired her for an event.

As she gave him the card, her fingers brushed his. No sparks, but her skin heated where they'd touched. Rachael forced herself not to shake her hand so it would feel normal again. "It's nice to meet you."

"Same." Mason's cheeks reddened.

The unexpected reaction was adorable for a man wearing a designer tux that likely cost as much as her car. He might be one of the tech billionaires. The tall one—Dash—had seemed geekier than the others, including Mason. But his blush made her wonder. Was that what he usually did? Or had he experienced the same burst of heat when they touched?

He glanced at the card and placed it in his jacket pocket. "Thanks."

"You're welcome."

Who was she kidding? He probably had felt nothing. Still, her gaze lingered on him. No wedding band on his left hand, but some men didn't wear rings. She hadn't seen him with a date, though.

Stop.

His relationship status didn't matter.

Even if he'd felt the same heat as her, Rachael wouldn't flirt with a guest, especially one who might be a potential client.

Besides, it wasn't as if a billionaire would be interested in someone like her. Well, not in a way she would agree to.

She turned her attention to Henry. "You mentioned the next wedding. Is someone engaged?"

A glance passed between Adam, Henry, and Mason. She had no way to translate the unspoken conversation happening among the trio, but it was curious.

"No, but Kieran caught the garter tonight." Henry glanced over his shoulder at the man who wore the garter on his arm and danced with others. "That means he'll be next."

"Henry believes in traditions." Mason's stare intensified.

Uncomfortable, she shifted her weight between her feet. Once men realized she was hired help, their attention usually changed. Some expected her to offer other…services after an event finished. Would Mason?

"I do." Henry made a sour face. "But I draw the line at sleeping with a piece of cake under my pillow. That tradition is too messy even with a live-in housekeeper."

"Messy, yes, but not if you put the plate with the cake into a gallon-sized plastic bag." Rachael had suggested that to a maid of honor, who was the only unmarried member of the wedding party last winter. "For some, that's a good trade-off for the chance to dream of your future spouse."

Adam rolled his eyes. "If Henry wanted a wife."

"Henry's never getting married," Mason chimed in.

"That's correct. Matrimony and I have an agreement. We're two ships which shall only pass in the night." Henry held his head high. "So, tradition or not, there's no need for me to sleep on the cake. But perhaps we should tell Kieran to do that."

Mason laughed. "Tradition doesn't mean certainty."

Adam held up his left hand to show the platinum band on his ring finger. "I never caught a garter, yet here I am."

"Your wedded bliss is the perfect blend of my matchmaking and Mother Nature's efforts." Henry's mouth quirked. He glanced around the venue. "Though I don't believe Kieran's perfect woman is here tonight, so the cake might come in handy. If not, I will join in the search. I won't give up until I find her."

"Give up for all of our sakes, please," Mason muttered under his breath.

That piqued her curiosity. With his money and looks, he would have no trouble finding dates. None of these men would. Rachael should let it go, but she had to ask. "Not a fan of marriage?"

"The institution is fine for people like Adam and Cambria." Mason didn't hesitate to answer. "But it's not for me. At least not at the moment, or say, the next five or ten years. I'm too busy with work."

"That's your choice," Henry said.

Mason nodded. "And I'll continue making the same choice."

"For now." Adam's tone held a hint of mystery.

Whatever he'd meant, Cambria agreed.

"I understand making your career a priority. That's what I'm doing." Rachael doubted Mason needed defending, but she felt the same way. "It's difficult having your focus pulled in too many directions."

"Exactly," Mason said.

"Once you fall in love, it's easier to figure out your priorities. Work drops lower on the list." Adam brushed his lips across Cambria's. "You know what they say…"

"When you know, you know," Henry and Cambria repeated at the same time. The two laughed.

"That was true in your case," Cambria said to Adam.

"You mean our case." Adam kissed the top of her hand.

Mason made an exaggerated face. "I need something to counteract all this sweetness. I'm surprised violins or a cherub with a harp aren't playing."

Henry sighed. "It's about time you nerds fell in love. Well, one of you."

"The best one." Adam beamed.

Affection flowed from one man to the other. If not for their different coloring and features, Rachael would think they were brothers. She envied having that kind of closeness with a group of people outside her immediate family.

Her chest tightened.

Someday, she would have that. Her gaze strayed to Mason, who was watching her.

She cleared her throat. "I need to speak to the photographers. It was nice chatting again, Henry, and meeting you, Mason."

"The pleasure was mine." Mason's gaze held hers once again, and flutters filled her stomach. Those gold flecks in his eyes lit up, capturing her attention, making it impossible for her to look away.

So not good.

Rachael had her reputation to consider. And her father's. She was nothing like him. Whatever she did, she would prove that to people. That meant not flirting or doing anything that would shine a negative light on her business.

Or her.

Time to stop standing around. She had work to do.

She forced a wide smile, making her facial muscles hurt.

"Enjoy the rest of the reception, everyone."

With that, she hurried away from the group.

Rachael was tempted to glance over her shoulder at Mason, but she controlled the urge. Nothing would throw her off-balance while she worked.

Not even a hottie billionaire.

Chapter Three

After the bride and groom departed, the bartender announced the last call. The reception wound down fast after that, but smiles never wavered. As SUVs drove guests to the lodge, where some would spend the night and others would head to accommodations in nearby Hood Hamlet or home, Rachael remained at the Silcox Hut.

The staff cleaned up, so Rachael had little to do once she collected and boxed her things. She would give a few items to the couple when they returned from their honeymoon. Others would go in her party stash for future events.

She walked around the main room and into where the bride dressed before the ceremony to make sure everything had been picked up. Nothing was there.

And that meant one thing.

Her day was almost finished.

A glance at the time showed five after midnight. Rachael might make it home before two. She yawned before stretching, hoping to loosen her tight and tired muscles.

"Hey."

She jumped, her hand flying to her chest.

"I'm sorry if I startled you," a male voice said.

She turned to see Mason Reese. No flutters this time, but her skin tingled. "I didn't realize anyone was here besides the staff, and I haven't seen them for a few minutes."

"I was down at the lodge, but I thought I'd forgotten my bowtie. I caught a ride in one of the SUVs coming up."

Rachael noticed his bowtie was missing. "Did you find it?"

"Turns out, Henry picked it up for me and forgot to tell me."

"Sorry you wasted a trip."

"Not wasted."

Because?

But she wasn't brave enough to ask.

Mason tilted his head. "The lodge is noisy. The quiet is…nice."

Okay, the silence was what made him happy, not seeing her. She shouldn't be surprised. If he were as wealthy as Adam and Henry, Mason wouldn't be interested in someone like her. "It was quiet like this when I arrived earlier. I love the stillness."

"Do you want to get married here?"

"I…" The question surprised her, but then again, she planned weddings, so people sometimes wondered what she wanted on her big day. "It's a lovely location and perfect for many couples, but…probably not. An occupational hazard of my line of work is imagining your own events. I picture my wedding at a bigger venue and out in the country, not on a mountain."

"Like a barn?"

"If it were a nice barn. Most likely, a winery, but I'm not dating anyone, so I have plenty of time to figure it out."

Not subtle at all. Rachael forced herself not to cringe.

He raised an eyebrow. The gesture might have looked ridiculous on another man, but it added to his appeal. She swallowed.

"The event planner doesn't have a plan?" he asked.

She laughed, her muscles twitching and her heart beating faster. She wanted to take a step toward him at the same time she wanted to retreat.

Weird. That hadn't happened to her before.

"Unfortunately, you can't plan to fall in love." As she pictured Cambria and Adam, warmth balled at the center of Rachael's chest. "Most of my clients say the same thing— love happens when you least expect it. Planning for it would be a waste of time. And that's a valuable and precious commodity right now."

"It is." Mason kept his gaze on her.

Rachael's body temperature rose, and she didn't like it.

"Do you need any help?" he asked.

"No, thanks. I'm finished."

"Is the box yours?"

"Yes."

He picked up the box from the table. "I'll carry this outside for you."

"Thanks." Rachael wasn't about to turn down free labor. She put on a lightweight jacket and grabbed her leather tote, which doubled as a purse at events so she could bring emergency supplies and extra items she might need.

Outside, the temperature had dropped since saying goodbye to the bride and the groom. But the cold didn't bother her, not with millions of stars twinkling in the night sky. A few pinpricks of light appeared to be close enough to touch. "It's beautiful."

"It is. I forget how the city lights interfere with seeing stars."

"My apartment view is of another building, so this is a huge improvement."

"Do you live in Portland?"

"Yes." Her studio was far from posh, but the rent was affordable. It also came with a private garage where she stored items for her business. "How about you?"

"I live in Portland, too."

Probably not the same area as her. Oh, her neighborhood wasn't bad, per se. Borderline sketchy after a particular time at night, which didn't make her feel comfortable when events ran late, but so far, she'd had no issues.

"Is your office in Portland?" he asked.

No office. Not yet, anyway. She met with clients at curated places such as coffee houses or cafés, where she knew the atmosphere would be suitable for discussing events, but not amazing where they might choose to hold something there without her help. "I'm looking for space."

Which was true.

Only, Rachael hadn't found one that fit her budget, but she scoured the listings each day. Given her business's name, she wanted to be in a trendier area, which meant higher rents. So far, her clients didn't appear to mind where they met.

"My friends keep telling me to buy a house, but I don't have the time to look." Mason walked next to her on the way to the SUV, shortening his stride to match hers. "Especially when my loft is all I need."

A loft in Portland wouldn't be cheap. A billionaire might also define loft differently from her. He might live in the same city, but he occupied a different galaxy from her.

A lodge employee opened the rear passenger door of the SUV, and she climbed in. She glanced over her shoulder. "Thank you."

The guy took the box from Mason. "I've got this."

"Thanks." Mason sat next to her, so close his thigh touched hers.

Heat emanated from the point of contact, similar to when their hands touched earlier, and she tried to ignore it.

Tired.

The long day had exhausted her. That explained why she was so…so hypersensitive around him. She stared at the driver's headrest.

Even not looking at Mason, she was aware of him. It wasn't only from where he touched her. The SUV's interior closed in on her as if shrinking with each passing second, despite only the two of them as passengers. That had nothing to do with how she felt and everything to do with the man next to her.

Don't think about him.

The driver slid into the vehicle. "The others aren't ready

to leave yet. I'll drop you off now."

"Thanks for not making us wait," Mason said before she could.

"Yes, thank you." She wouldn't have wanted to be stuck here any longer with a drive home still ahead of her.

The drive went by fast. Neither of them spoke. Country music played on the radio, but she couldn't have named one song.

Rachael covered her mouth and yawned again. This was becoming a habit.

"Are you staying at the lodge tonight, too?" Mason asked.

"No. I'm driving home."

As the corners of his mouth turned downward, his brows drew together. "Would you like to grab a cup of coffee before you take off?"

Her yawn must have worried him, which was sweet of him but unnecessary. "Thanks, but I have an event tomorrow morning, so I have to hit the road."

"Another wedding?"

"A baby shower brunch." Rachael pictured the boxes she'd prepared yesterday for the event. She'd wanted to have everything ready to go. "I need sleep, or I'll be a zombie tomorrow. My clients deserve better than that."

"Your clients are fortunate you care so much."

"Thank you. I try to give my all."

"That's clear." Mason hesitated. "I was wondering… Could we meet for coffee? Say Monday afternoon?"

She memorized her schedule three days at a time, so she

didn't need to glance at the calendar on her phone. "I'm meeting with a client."

"You're busy."

Rachael nodded. "I'm working hard to grow my business."

"Well, if today is any indication, you'll succeed."

"Thanks." He was so complimentary—and hot. If he wanted to discuss an event, she needed to forget about what he looked like. "I'm free on Tuesday afternoon if that day works for you."

"It does," he sputtered and brushed his fingers through his hair. "I have your card. I'll text you on Monday to firm up the details."

She stifled a yawn. "Okay."

The van stopped at the lodge. "I'll take you to your car, miss."

"Thank you." Rachael glanced at Mason, who remained seated. "Enjoy the rest of your weekend."

His lips slanted. "Are you up to driving home tonight?"

He was sweet. That was surprising but nice. "I'll be fine. Thanks."

Mason's gaze locked on hers. He moved closer to her as if he wanted to kiss her before he stiffened, his posture going ramrod straight.

"Be careful on your way home." He hopped out of the SUV and glanced over his shoulder. "Good night."

Before she could reply, he walked to the lodge's entrance.

She watched him go until the SUV turned toward the parking lot.

Rachael half laughed. Her imagination and tiredness had turned a simple moment into an almost-kiss. She should grab a coffee on her way out of town. The caffeine would wake her up and clear her head for the drive.

Uh-oh. She hadn't asked Mason what kind of event he wanted to discuss.

Oh, well. Rachael would wing it, which was a skill she'd honed since she was a teenager.

Chapter Four

On Tuesday, Mason stood outside a coffee shop, half a block from the trendy NW 23rd Avenue. The temperature hovered around ninety. Sweat beaded at his hairline and ran down his neck. He'd ditched his suit jacket the minute he'd entered his office this morning, but even if he'd been in a T-shirt and shorts, the hot weather would be uncomfortable. If only the heat were the only reason. He undid the two top buttons on his shirt.

The coffee shop's glass door loomed in front of him, challenging him to enter.

He'd left work early—a rarity on the caliber of a hurricane in Portland—and now he regretted doing that.

Still, he should go inside. Rachael might be waiting for him.

Who am I kidding?

She was, or she would expect him to be there when she arrived.

So why did he want to turn around, get in his car, and drive to his office?

Because something about her intrigued him in a way nothing but lines of code or his growing net worth had in years. She'd been on his mind since Saturday's wedding.

His invitation for coffee wasn't premeditated. He hadn't wanted to say goodbye at the lodge, but Rachael hadn't been able to stay, so asking her out had seemed like the best option.

Now he wasn't so sure.

That was unlike him.

Mason Reese didn't hesitate. He saw an opportunity and went for it. That was how TVT, his company, had been created.

His uncertainty and wanting to bail was…strange. He had things to discuss with her, including improvements to her website. On Sunday, he'd stalked her. Okay, late Saturday night instead of meeting his friends at the bar, but it had been after midnight, so technically the next day.

He would email her his list of suggestions when he got to the office. A ton of work awaited him there. That was more important than his curiosity about the posh planner.

His interest in her was just that—curiosity.

It had nothing to do with Rachael's warm smile or how her clear green eyes reminded him of the park where he used to play as a kid or that her laugh had become his new favorite sound.

Yep, Mason was acting like one of his mom's curious cats.

Except he only had one life, not nine.

Time to get out of here.

"Mason."

Recognizing Rachael's voice behind him, his muscles tensed. So much for leaving. He'd spent too much time deciding what to do. He forced a grin before turning. "Hey."

"Sorry, I'm late."

Stray strands of hair from her ponytail framed her face perfectly. Her floral-print skirt fell above her knees, showing off her legs. The short-sleeved peach shirt complemented her complexion. Pink tinged her cheeks, suggesting she'd been hurrying.

Had she gotten prettier since Saturday night?

"I had to pick up something," she added.

"I'm early." The words rushed out.

Chill, Reese. Don't act like Dash.

He opened the door, not wanting to make either of them suffer in the heat any longer. "After you."

As she passed by, a citrus fragrance tickled his nose. Her shampoo? Soap? He hadn't smelled that on Saturday night when they sat next to each other in the SUV.

Not that how she smelled mattered.

Mason forced his attention off her and onto the place. The shop wasn't a massive franchise but a locally owned coffee house Rachael had suggested. He understood why. The cozy atmosphere with subdued lighting and soft instrumental jazz playing was an excellent setting for a first date. Mason joined her in line.

"What would you like?" they asked at the same time.

She laughed. "Let's try that again. What do you want?"

Wait. Was she offering to buy his coffee? "This is my

treat. I asked you to meet me."

She studied the menu board. "Yes, but this is what I always do."

Huh? He supposed some women might prefer paying, but he wasn't used to that. Most expected him to pay, given his net worth. A few even hinted about the expensive gifts they wanted. But Rachael seemed genuine in her offer, so he would let her. "An iced coffee, please."

"Anything to eat?"

"No, thanks. I had a late lunch with Kieran and Henry."

"They both seem nice."

"They are." Henry had his moments, though. Tonight, they would talk about getting Kieran together with Selah, who worked for Mason. If the two got married, there would be one less person in the bet.

Rachael stepped up to the counter and removed her wallet from the light-blue purse on her wrist. "One iced tea and an iced coffee for here."

The barista, a woman with pink hair, rang up the order. "Someone will bring those to you in a few minutes."

"Thanks." Rachael handed over a twenty-dollar bill, placed two dollars into the tip jar, and tucked the change and receipt in her wallet. She glanced at him. "Let's find a place to sit."

The coffee house was quiet. Only a few tables were taken.

Mason noticed a small round table for two that was more secluded than the others and gave them some privacy. "How about the one in the corner?"

"Perfect." She headed there and sat. "I hope you've had a wonderful week so far."

"Fairly typical." That meant crazy busy, but Mason thrived on that. "Did your baby shower go well?"

Rachael's face lit up. "It did. The mother-to-be was so sweet, and everyone had fun."

"You love what you do."

She nodded. "Each client is special to me. It may sound corny, but I'm grateful to be a part of whatever event they're celebrating."

Once again, her genuineness struck him. "That's sweet."

"It's also selfish. None of my family lives in Oregon, so it's almost like being a member of someone else's family for a few hours."

Her wistful expression hit him hard. She must miss her family.

Whereas Mason managed a weekly call to his parents. He stared at the table, hoping to find something to snag his attention, but nothing was there. He shifted in the chair. "I rarely see my family, and they live in the same state."

"It's hard to make time when you're so busy."

He didn't know if she was talking about him or herself. Perhaps both. He would rather they discuss her. "Do you work most weekends?"

"It depends on my client's needs. This last weekend I worked both days. But I only have one this Saturday."

A Saturday night date was out of the question. If—and that was a big if—he wanted to invite her out. Despite his freakout on the sidewalk, he kind of did. "So, you aren't fully booked?"

"No. That gives me flexibility for clients like Cambria and Adam, who don't have a lot of lead time."

"That's smart." Mason was glad she'd fit the wedding in, or he would have never met her. "Henry says your business is going well."

With a satisfied smile on her face, Rachael sat taller. "It is. We're growing, but…"

"It's never enough."

"Exactly."

Laughter lit her eyes, and his heart bumped. She was so beautiful.

"I have big dreams. Goals," she added.

He never expected to be so captivated, but he was. That should bother him more than it did.

"I know how that goes." Mason was glad he hadn't left earlier. "And after you hit those initial ones, you want to reach for the next."

She leaned slightly over the table. "Is that what you're doing?"

He nodded. "But developing a follow-up to a popular product is…challenging."

"That's part of the appeal, right?"

"Guilty." He half laughed. "Don't get me wrong. I've got nothing against easy, and I love when things click into place, but much of the creative process happens when I'm trying to overcome obstacles and problems. That's how I ended up developing TVT."

"I love your app, and so does everyone I know. I'm glad you made it."

His chest swelled. "Thank you. We're working on an update now. It'll be even better."

The barista carried their drinks on a tray. She placed each on the table. "Enjoy."

As he picked up his, the glass was cool against his palm. "Thanks for this."

"My pleasure." Rachael took a sip of hers. "I know you're busy, and I don't want to take too much of your time today. So, what kind of event are you having?"

He froze, holding his iced coffee halfway to his mouth. "Event?"

She nodded, which told him nothing. "I have brochures, and a few packages are listed on my website to give clients ideas, but most of my events are custom, which is why I love doing consultations like this. It helps me put together exactly what a client needs."

Consultation. Client.

The word swirled inside his mind, mocking him.

She thought I invited her to talk about an event, not a date.

Mason almost laughed. He placed his drink on the table so he didn't spill any.

No wonder she'd paid for his coffee.

Henry might be correct when he claimed Mason had no skills talking to women. He'd epically failed with Rachael.

She appeared eager for more business. He didn't want to let her down. "I'm not sure."

That was true.

Again, Mason kept himself from laughing. He hadn't been looking to date anyone, but he wouldn't deny his attraction to Rachael. Perhaps working with her would be a way to get to know her without the pressure of going out and more awkwardness, like her not realizing he thought this was a date.

She'd mentioned having her wedding in the country. She might enjoy planning an event there. "What do you think of a party at a winery?"

Her sparkling eyes matched her wide grin. "That would be fun."

"It would." Especially the planning portion with her. He and his friends hired Iris when they hosted parties at their homes, but this would be different.

Bigger.

"My friends enjoy wine." Especially Henry, who had stocked Mason's wine collection for him. "A meal with a wine tasting could work. Or something like that."

"Do you want it near Portland or where people would spend the night?" As she tapped her chin, her gaze turned hazy as if looking off into the distance. But the only thing in front of her was a brick wall. She straightened. "A party bus might be a good idea, depending on the location."

Mason could fly people to a chateau in France for the night if he wanted. A party bus or limousine rental would be nothing. "What do you suggest?"

She tilted her head as if deep in thought. "The Willamette Valley has some gorgeous wineries with event spaces. Even though many are driving distance, with alcohol served, I would suggest offering overnight suggestions and rides to and from, giving your guests options."

"I'll pay for both the hotel rooms and transportation. That way, people don't have to worry about the cost."

His closest friends could afford it, but not everyone else was in the same position.

She pulled out a tablet. "Do you have a date in mind?"

Until a few minutes ago, he didn't know he would host an event. It was now July. A month or two working together might be nice. "Do you have any availability in September?"

"I do." She glanced up from her phone. Her eyes twinkled. "If you're not set on a date, I suggest you wait to pick one until I see the availability of venues."

"I'm completely flexible." Warmth spread through him. One good thing about having so much money was he could spend it on whatever he wanted. A party would be a worthy expense, especially if it helped Rachael build her business and gave him a reason to spend more time with her. A second event by another billionaire of Silicon Forest would give her buzz. He could invite people who needed event planners. Henry would know who else Mason should include.

"How many people?" Her serious tone matched her expression.

"I'm working on the guest list." He didn't want to be too specific since he was clueless about what the event would entail. "Look for a venue, and we can work from there based on the occupancy limits."

"That's an excellent idea." She typed on her phone. "Do you want to visit the places in person or check them out online?"

"In-person, please. Once we have a shortlist, we can visit

those." His chest puffed—best plan ever. A date visiting wineries would be ideal. Well, not officially a date. But they would be together. That was close to the same thing, right?

"Perfect."

Yes, this would be perfect. "I'm not worried about the budget. This party will be a splurge."

Her lips parted, matching her wide eyes.

Oh, yes. Rachael would have fun planning his event. He would be the perfect client, so she would never forget him.

"Don't let the cost deter you," he continued. "Tell me your idea, and we can decide if the expense is worthwhile."

"Okay." She sounded as shocked as she looked. "I can do that."

"I trust you." For some unknown reason, Mason did, which was strange because his trust had become something others needed to earn. He'd learned that lesson many times over the years. Yet with Rachael, he would gladly hand it over, no questions asked.

Gratitude filled her gleaming eyes. "Thank you."

"No, thank you for helping me out." He picked up his drink. "So now that we've got the business stuff out of the way, tell me more about yourself. You mentioned your family isn't in Portland."

She sipped from her drink. "I'm from San Francisco."

"What brought you to the Pacific Northwest?"

Rachael bit her lip, hesitating. "Portland is growing, and I thought it would be a better place to start…start my business."

"Makes sense."

"Are you from Portland?" she asked.

"I grew up in Bend. I met Wes and Kieran at a conference when I was in college. Both convinced me the Silicon Forest was a good place to found a company. Lower cost of living than the Bay Area and plenty of skilled employees here."

She nodded. "It's a great place to live."

Especially with her there. Working with Rachael on a party gave him an idea for something his friend Kieran should do with Selah. *Yes.* Mason sipped his drink. Everything would work out brilliantly.

Chapter Five

Sitting next to Mason in the limousine on Sunday, Rachael fought the urge to run her fingertips along the soft leather. The upholstery was nicer than her couch. Who was she kidding? The car was better than her apartment. A good thing she'd had Mason pick her up in front of a coffee shop in a trendier neighborhood than hers.

She inhaled, wanting another sniff of what she could only call the scent of money in the air. She'd named her business The Posh Planner, but that was only branding. Everything else about her was bargain basement, thrift stores, or consignment shop finds.

Okay, she was doing better than that these days. Her company planned posh events, so the name wasn't a pretense, but she hoped to live up to her brand in every sense of her lifestyle.

Someday.

Even though her fingers itched to touch all the buttons and switches within reach of her arm, Rachael ignored them. She didn't want Mason to think she had never ridden in a limo before. She had, but it had been years ago. Her parents' chauffeur, Claude, had been more like a doting uncle than a family employee. He'd been a part of her life for as long as she remembered. Until her father's gambling habit wiped away her safe, comfortable world, leaving her without friends or a place to call home. At least she didn't have to worry about that now.

Mason stretched out his feet. "I enjoy not having to drive."

She glanced out the window. The rolling hills of vineyards greeted her, reminding her of family picnics at vineyards in Napa. That seemed like forever ago. "It was nice of Henry to loan you his car and driver."

"That's what friends are for."

Someday, she hoped to make friends like that. Oh, she didn't care if they had limos or money. But she wanted to surround herself with helpful, caring, and compassionate people. Having only herself to rely upon got tiring. "You seem close to yours."

"I am." Mason's grin spread. "We met when I was starting out. The others were in a similar position, except for Wes and Henry, who both had family money. But we were trying to make our marks."

"You all succeeded."

Mason nodded. "We won't let each other fail."

"Must be nice to have that support."

"It is. And it's nice to be spending today with you."

So far, they'd visited two wineries. Mason hadn't given her much to go on about venues, but each stop taught her more about him and what he wanted. He might be a tech billionaire, but he was easygoing. Not once had he glanced at his phone, which surprised her. He asked her opinion, more so than other clients. She thought that must be because he was here on his own. No fiancée, significant other, or a friend to ask. She didn't mind, but she had to remind herself this wasn't her event. They weren't a couple, and she was only his planner.

That had never happened before.

Mason also preferred opening the car door for her rather than waiting for Frank. It would be so easy to consider today a date.

Stop being ridiculous.

This was business. Nothing else. *Except…*

She stared at the space between them. The distance had shrunk because his hand nearly touched hers. If she moved her pinky a half-inch—

Focus. Rachael raised her gaze. "What did you think of the last place?"

"Nice, but it felt a little too…"

"French Chateau?" she offered.

He nodded. "I don't want rustic with dirt floors, but something in between might be nice."

That would have been helpful info to know ahead of time, but he might have only figured out what he wanted after seeing the first two places. "The next winery fits that description."

"I look forward to seeing it." As he raised his hand, his finger brushed hers.

Tingles skittered up her hand to her arm.

Mason motioned to the bar. "Do you want anything to drink?"

"No, thanks." Each place had offered glasses of wine, but she'd declined since she was working. "But don't let me stop you."

"I'm fine." He returned his hand to the spot next to hers. Even closer this time.

It means nothing.

"What's the name of the next winery?" he asked.

Rachael forced her gaze off their hands. "Welton Wineries. It's family-owned."

"Wait." His forehead creased. "Welton Wines and Chocolate in Hood Hamlet?"

"That's a satellite shop run by the owners' grandsons. Have you been there?"

"Yes, Henry—and Wes, who was also at the wedding— have vacation homes in Hood Hamlet." Mason's words came faster. He leaned toward her. "I've done wine and chocolate tastings at the shop. Both were fantastic."

"The winery has a lovely event venue. I put my name on their waitlist for September on Tuesday evening. A good thing I did because I got a call yesterday that someone canceled their event on the first Saturday in September. Though, the date might be too soon for you."

"No, that would be fine." He straightened. "If I like the place."

"If not, there's more we can look at." Clients rarely visited a venue and declared it the one. Well, except Cambria and Adam, but they'd had specific criteria for Rachael that made the search easier.

Mason stretched out his legs. "I'm torn about whether or not I want to like this next one."

"Why?"

"I want to find a venue, but spending another day in the wine country wouldn't suck."

She laughed. "Would you be working today if you weren't here?"

"Possibly. Though, if it were exhibition season or fall, I'd be with my friends, watching football."

His friends—the Billionaires of Silicon Forest, Henry Davenport, and Brett Matthews. She had college friends and sorority sisters, but she'd heard Henry and Brett had grown up together. Henry and Wes, too. All her friends from high school no longer spoke to her. They hadn't since her family lost everything, which meant they hadn't been her friends despite saying they were.

She shook off the truth. "That must be fun."

"It is." Mason touched the top of her hand. "But there's nowhere else I'd rather be today."

Her mouth went dry. She cleared her throat.

"Thanks." Rachael's voice sounded shaky. She didn't know what else to say, but the silence made her want to squirm. "I'm excited to plan an event at a winery."

"So…" As Mason lifted his hand off hers, he angled his shoulders toward Rachael. "You've asked me questions. Now, it's my turn."

"What do you want to know?"

His gaze sharpened. "More about you."

"My business?"

"Yes, but also you outside of The Posh Planner."

Rachael gulped. She didn't talk about herself. Well, not much beyond her company and recent past. It was easier—safer—that way. She'd been a kid and not responsible for her dad's gambling and the subsequent losses, both personal and professional. Still, people had treated her entire family as if they'd all been at fault, so she stopped saying anything to keep from being judged.

"Well, I'm not used to riding in limousines." By tomorrow, the scent of money tickling her nose would only be a dream. "This is a special treat."

"Henry wants me to buy one, but I doubt I would use a limousine enough. I enjoy driving."

"If you ever need a ride, there are plenty of ride-share apps, too, but I can see how limousines came in handy before those existed."

"Tell me something else."

Thankfully, her father hadn't been able to touch her college fund, or who knows where she'd be today. "I graduated with a degree in hospitality business management from Washington State University. I spent my summers working in restaurants and hotels to learn all I could. The Posh Planner is the result."

Her parents hated that Rachael had graduated from a state school, and one in Eastern Washington, instead of an elite private university, but she didn't care because the college had her major and was more affordable. The truth was, she hadn't seen them in years. It was as much them as it was her, but she wouldn't enable her dad's gambling addiction. As soon as things appeared to turn around for her parents, he returned to his old habits. No way would she allow him to take more from her than he already had.

But a few hours with Mason brought back the world of wealth and privilege her father had lost for them. She might put on expensive events for wealthy people, but she was nothing more than a hired hand to make sure everything turned out well.

Today, she felt as feted as Mason by the wineries, hoping to be his venue of choice. It was…nice.

The limousine turned into the entrance for Welton Wineries. Thank goodness they were here because Rachael didn't want to talk about herself.

Staring out the window, she saw the building that housed the tasting room. It was gorgeous with wood and stone details. She'd never visited their event facility, but the photos of the various buildings—including the "ballroom" with a vaulted beamed ceiling—on their website appealed to her on a gut level.

"This is our next stop." She hoped this was more of what Mason wanted. "Let's see what you think of this one."

* * *

This is more like it.

Mason surveyed the room that was larger than he needed for the dinner, but they'd assured him it could feel intimate if he desired that. He had no idea what they would do, but the wood floors and wood beams on the ceilings and the gigantic stone fireplace gave the space character that made people take a second look. "The glass doors let in sunlight and showed off the fountain outside."

Kaitlyn Welton, a pretty woman in her early twenties, opened a door. "When the weather's nice, we can open or remove the doors if you prefer a more outdoor feel. If you want something both indoors and outdoors, the patio is the perfect spot for cocktails and appetizers."

"The patio would be a nice location for appetizers before your dinner." Rachael buzzed with excitement. She wasn't as wiggly as a kid in a candy shop, but her step had more of a bounce than it had at the first two wineries. She bit her lip before raising her gaze to his. "What do you think?"

The hope in her voice matched the gleam in her eyes. She was adorable.

Seeing her happy pleased him. He wanted to keep that beautiful smile on her face. "It's perfect. I'd love to have my dinner here."

Rachael clapped her hands together. "Wonderful. The décor can be rustic or elegant or a combination, whichever you prefer."

He loved her enthusiasm. "I trust your judgment."

Mason did. He didn't know what putting on an event involved. His idea was to let her do as she wanted. Henry offered to make up the guest list since they ran in similar circles. All Mason had to do was provide the names of people associated with TVT he wanted to include since Henry might not know them. The only thing left for Mason to do was pay for everything, which was the easiest part. If everything worked out as he planned—and it usually did—his dinner would give Rachel's business much-needed exposure and new clients.

"I've prepared a small tasting for you in the main winery. I'll grab the contract. We can talk in there," Kaitlyn said. "Look around on your own before you make your way over."

"Thank you." Mason waited until Kaitlyn left. Rachael's expression told him what her answer would be, but he still wanted to ask. "You like this one as much as I do, right?"

"I love it." She spun around as if wanting a three-hundred-and-sixty-degree look. "But you're the one who needs to love it…"

Love wasn't a word he used often, but he loved she was so happy with the winery. "I do, too. It's bigger than I thought it would be, so we could have dancing."

She pulled out her tablet. "Do you prefer a DJ or a band?"

"Which would you want?"

"It depends on who is available. I can put together a short list for you."

"Sounds good."

A wistful expression formed on her face.

"What?" he asked.

"I was thinking about the weddings I saw in the winery's event portfolio."

A wedding wasn't on his five- or ten-year plans, but even

he saw the appeal to Rachael. "Maybe you'll get married here someday."

She beamed. "Maybe."

As he imagined her dancing with her groom, Mason's insides twisted. Talk about a strange reaction. "Have you seen enough?"

Rachael nodded. "I'm sure they have a folder of information, including measurements."

"Did you bring a tape measure?"

"I did." She patted her purse. "I always carry one with me."

"Prepared."

"I have to be." Rachael typed on her tablet before glancing up at him. "Otherwise, I wouldn't be in business long."

"I have a feeling your business is going to soar."

She shimmied her shoulders. "Thanks. I sure hope so."

The Posh Planner didn't need hope or even luck. Mason grinned. Not when she had him on her side.

Chapter Six

On Wednesday evening, Mason sat at a conference table surrounded by his top-level executives who kept TVT running. He hated keeping them late. But with Selah working at Kieran's company in the mornings, this was the only time to get everyone together. Not that he had anything for them this week, but a few had items for him. All he needed was to pay attention. Someone else—okay, Selah—took notes, so he didn't need to jot anything down.

The only problem?

Mason's mind was on Rachael.

The same place it had been since saying goodbye on Sunday afternoon. He replayed wanting to ask her to dinner to celebrate finding a location for his party, but before he could, Rachael told him she had to work on an upcoming luncheon, so he hadn't. Instead, they'd texted about the next steps. She'd mentioned driving to Salem, an hour away, today to have lunch with a friend, so he'd messaged her around one o'clock about getting together to discuss the upcoming dinner as the reason, but she hadn't replied. That had been hours ago.

She'd always gotten back to him quicker in the past.

He didn't remember her talking about an event tonight. He'd checked her website to see her calendar for potential clients listed under her availability, but today was empty.

So, where was she?

The question gnawed at his gut.

Salem wasn't that far. She should be home by now.

Scenarios swirled, from a migraine—not that she'd mentioned having them—to an accident on I-5, to her being kidnapped ran through his head. Mason didn't know where she lived. He'd picked her up and dropped her off in front of a coffee shop. He assumed she lived nearby, but that didn't give him anything to go on.

Not that he would if he had more info about her.

Or should.

Checking her calendar was borderline stalkerish. But he was concerned. She was usually prompt in replying to him.

Dash could help. The guy had mad hacker skills, even if he denied using them as much as he did when he was younger. As if twenty-eight was old. All Mason had to do was ask.

"Is there anything else you want to know?" Selah's voice jolted Mason. He had no idea what they'd been discussing.

"No."

The others appeared relieved. He was. Rachael's phone might have died. He would call her again and see if her voice mail picked up this time.

"Thanks for staying late today." He pushed away from the table. "I'll see you tomorrow."

His executive team hurried out of the room. Mason didn't blame them. If he had someone waiting at home for him, he would rush out, too. Once again, he glanced at his phone.

"Are you expecting a call?" Selah asked.

Busted. Heat pooled on his face. "A reply to a text."

There wasn't anything else he could say. Selah knew him well enough to see through any lies, too.

Her gaze narrowed. "You were distracted during the meeting."

"Did I miss much?"

Selah rolled her eyes. "I'll send you the notes tonight and recap any key points."

"Thanks."

A test notification sounded. He glanced at his phone, but it was from Blaise in their group chat. Not—

Selah studied him. "Based on your expression, that wasn't the reply you wanted."

"No."

"Must be important."

He shrugged. "I thought I'd hear from someone by now."

"Someone? Or a woman?"

Selah was too perceptive. Then again, she'd known him since he was nineteen. "A woman, but not like you're thinking. I hired her."

Selah raised an eyebrow. "This gets curiouser and curiouser."

"She's planning a dinner for me."

"Tonight?"

"September."

"You rarely plan like that."

Selah was correct. He shrugged. "I'm helping an event planner I met at Adam's wedding."

"She must be pretty."

"Gorgeous." Mason caught himself. "I mean. She's nice and working hard to grow her business. My event will give her some exposure."

Laughter lit Selah's eyes. "Sure, boss. Keep telling yourself that. But instead of waiting for her to call, reach out to her. You're a client, right?"

He straightened. "I am."

"So, call her. You're smart enough to have a question."

No, all he wanted to do was hear Rachael's voice, which told him not to call, to cancel the dinner, and to forget about her. Except he didn't want to do that, either. "I will."

As soon as he figured out what to say to Rachael that wouldn't make him sound like a complete idiot.

* * *

As Rachael unlocked the door to her apartment, she stifled a yawn. The opportunity to put on an impromptu cocktail party for a sorority sister's mom tonight had meant a non-stop afternoon to pull the appetizers and drinks together. Not to mention the decorations—mainly flowers and candles—with such little notice. Rachael was exhausted, but her friend, the mom, and the guests were thrilled. That made all her hard work worthwhile. The extra money in her business checking account didn't hurt, either.

Inside, Rachael kicked off her shoes, pulled out her cell phone, and tossed her bag on the counter. She'd turned off her phone earlier, but now the screen was dark. The battery must have died at some point today. She plugged in her charger before heading toward the bathroom.

A hot shower had her name on it.

Fifteen minutes later, she was clean and in her pajamas. She'd eaten a little at the party but needed more—even a bowl of cereal—to tide her over until morning. Otherwise, she'd wake up in the middle of the night starving.

As she filled a bowl with her sugary favorite containing miniature marshmallows, Rachael glanced at her phone. Notifications, texts, and voice mails filled her screen.

A glance showed her texts from Mason.

Oh, no. She hoped nothing was wrong.

Mason: *Hey, can we schedule a time to meet and discuss the dinner?*
Mason: *Not sure if you have an event, but could you call me?*
Mason: *Are you getting my texts?*
Mason: *Are you okay?*

The first message had arrived after lunch. Others were sent tonight. The last had been delivered when she was in the shower. Whatever he wanted to discuss must be important. She hoped he didn't cancel, but it wouldn't be the first time a client did that.

Unfortunately.

She checked her voice mail.

"Hey, Rachael. It's Mason. Mason Reese." Breathing filled the line. "I haven't heard from you, so I wanted to check in and see… Call me when you get this. Tonight. I'll be up late."

Funny, but he almost sounded concerned.

At least he hadn't canceled. Some clients expected fast replies. A billionaire probably did, too.

She dialed his number.

The phone barely rang, and the line connected.

"Rachael?" The name rushed out. "Everything okay?"

"It's fine. I had a last-minute booking, and my phone died at some point. I didn't have a charger. Sorry for not getting in touch sooner."

"You're okay."

It wasn't a question, but something in Mason's tone told her to answer.

"Tired and hungry after a long day, but otherwise, I'm great." She eyed the refrigerator, but her charge cord wouldn't stretch that far and the battery was still red. Her stomach would have to wait a few more minutes. "So you want to get together?"

"Yes. When are you free?" His words ran together. He must be working and in a rush.

"I have nothing going on until the weekend."

"Dinner tomorrow night."

"Sure, text me the address and time." She removed a box of cereal from the cabinet.

"I'll pick you up."

"You don't have to go out of your way."

"I don't mind."

She did. Mason didn't have a silver spoon upbringing like Henry Davenport and Wes Lockhart, who she'd met at Adam and Cambria's wedding, but a man worth as much as Mason Reese would take one look at where Rachael lived and pass judgment. He might not be wrong, but he also wouldn't be entirely correct about her. She wanted to avoid that.

"I need to eat," she added. "Text me where and when to meet, okay?"

He said nothing.

"Mason?" she asked.

"That's fine." His reluctant tone didn't match his words.

Weird. But perhaps all billionaires were eccentric. "Good night."

* * *

The next evening, Mason sat at the table with a flickering candle, a single rose in a bud vase, and a bottle of white wine chilling. She'd mentioned preferring white to red at one winery they'd visited. Everything was perfect for their dinner—everything except him.

Last night, fearing the worst about Rachael had been a game-changer.

He would have spent whatever it took to find her and make sure she was safe, healthy, happy.

Who am I kidding?

He'd wanted to do that since their first meeting at the coffee shop.

The only question—what did that mean?

Rachael hurried to the table. She wore a black skirt and a red tank top with strappy sandals. A small purse hung from her shoulder. "Sorry, I'm late. I couldn't find a parking spot."

"It's fine." He motioned to the wine bottle. "I ordered one of Welton's white wines."

She placed her purse strap around the chair and sat. "Our own tasting."

"That's what I was thinking." He poured her a glass. "How was your day?"

"Meetings with clients. Like now."

Mason bristled, not wanting her to see him as one more customer. He sipped from his glass.

"Only we didn't have food or wine or such a lovely setting." Her face brightened. "Thank you."

"You're welcome." Her earnest gratitude made him want to give her all the things, not only dinner tonight or an event to plan.

She scanned the menu before setting it on her plate.

"Know what you want?" he asked.

Rachael nodded. "What did you want to discuss about your dinner?"

"How about we enjoy our meal first?" he suggested. "We can get to know each other better and talk about the dinner party."

Lines creased her forehead. "Sure."

The topics of conversation ranged from favorite TV shows to fruit on a pizza to when they put up a Christmas tree or if they even had one. They only stopped talking when the server appeared to take their order and deliver their meals. Mason had never met anyone he'd clicked with so quickly.

Rachael wiped her mouth with a napkin. "This steak is amazing."

"So is the salmon." But nothing whetted his appetite as much as her.

A tension formed between his shoulder blades. The last thing he wanted was a girlfriend, but would just being friends with Rachael satisfy him?

No.

Maybe if he got to know her better, that would get her out of his system. But if that didn't work, where would that leave him? Them?

He hadn't a clue, but he never wanted to experience that sinking stomach, heart-in-his throat fear over her well-being again.

She raised her wineglass. "What are you thinking about?"

"You."

Her eyes widened.

He'd caught her off guard, but he didn't want to push too much. Not yet. "I'm glad we're having dinner."

"Me, too." She glanced around. "And great restaurant choice."

"It's one of my favorites. My friends and I come here a lot."

A corner of her mouth lifted in a cheeky grin. "The Billionaires of Silicon Forest?"

He laughed. "I can't believe that name stuck. The six of us are Adam, Blaise, Dash, Kieran, and Wes. Henry Davenport and Brett Matthews, who are honorary members, join us, too. They aren't in high tech, though Brett is a whiz with numbers and created his own investment program."

Her gaze met Mason's. "Well, I'm glad to be here with you. I love the atmosphere, the food, and the company."

Something shifted in his chest. She was the reason. That should scare him more than it did. "We've covered the first-date favorites."

Her forehead wrinkled. "The what?"

"The things you learn about someone when you go out for the first time. Favorite foods, colors, books."

Nodding, Rachael stared at her plate. She fingered the wineglass stem. "We've been out before, and this isn't—"

"Humor me." Mason leaned forward. "Look at me, please."

She did.

"We don't have to put a label on this."

"Your event—"

"Is going forward as we planned." He wanted to kiss away the concern in her eyes, but his words would have to do, given where they were at the moment. "Nothing will change that."

What appeared to be relief flashed on her face, but she remained silent.

"Let's see where this"—he pointed to her and then to himself—"goes."

"It might go nowhere." The words rushed out. Her cheeks reddened.

"True, or it could."

She lowered her gaze. "We're very different."

He grinned. "Are you trying to talk me out of this?"

She looked at him. "Maybe?"

"I haven't gotten where I am by giving up. Differences keep things interesting."

Rachael started to speak then stopped herself. She tucked her hair behind her ears. "So what happens next?"

That wasn't the resounding yes he'd hoped for, but he would take it. "We move beyond the surface-level conversation."

Her lower lip shot out in an adorable pout. "But I like knowing you love those sci-fi movies and TV shows, including the old ones. Or that the green on a hundred-dollar bill is your favorite color."

"And it's cute how you enjoy watching HGTV and The Great British Bake Off and believe no brunch is complete without mimosas."

Her face turned redder.

He loved seeing her blush. "But there's more we don't know, so now we open up. Share something few people know."

She leaned in her chair. "Do I need to sign an NDA first?"

Mason couldn't believe she offered, but it might be her business. Some clients probably required them. His lawyers would want him to say yes, but his net worth made things unequal between them. He didn't want to add another layer. "No, but I appreciate you asking. If you need me to sign one…"

It was Rachael's turn to laugh. "I wish…"

Mason wanted to give her everything she wanted—make all her wishes come true. The cost or the effort involved didn't matter.

She shifted in her chair. "You go first."

She was more hesitant about this than him. Plus, it had been his idea. "Everyone assumes I planned to start TVT since I was a kid, but that's not the case at all. Guess what I wanted to be when I was younger?"

She studied him. "A firefighter?"

"Good guess and most of my friends wanted to be one, but not me." His friends believed being a firefighter was not only the bravest job in the world but also the coolest. "I wanted to be a pizza maker."

Rachael grinned. "You love pizza."

Mason nodded. "Greatest food ever invented, but I loved the idea of making them for a living. I dreamed of tossing the crusts into the air and catching them."

Her face brightened. "How different your life would be if you'd become a pizza maker."

He pondered her words for a moment. "Different, yes, but who's saying I still wouldn't be a billionaire?"

Surprise flashed in her eyes. "You think?"

"Others have done it and become household names. Why not me, too?" Mason believed in himself—always had—even when others didn't. "My pizza would have been so delicious I would end up opening my own store. Add another and another until it became a franchise. Then I'd take it national and eventually global."

"This is why you're a billionaire, and I'm a business owner working out of her apartment." She half laughed. "Do you make pizza?"

"Only out of Play-Doh when I was younger. My mom was afraid I'd ruin her kitchen or set the house on fire, so I never had the chance. When I got older, it was easier to order one."

"Your mom ruined your pizza empire."

"Yes, but TVT hasn't been a bad backup plan. But if you want me to make you a pizza, I'm willing to learn. You can pick the toppings."

Her gaze met his.

Mason's heart thudded. He couldn't have looked away if he tried. But she didn't appear to be in any hurry, either. It was…nice.

Laughter from the table next to them filled the air. It was enough to break the mood and their connection.

He took another sip of wine. "Your turn."

She toyed with the edge of the tablecloth. "This is hard. I don't talk about anything private."

"You can trust me."

"I want to. It's just." She blew out a breath before sipping her wine. "Okay, here goes. I haven't spoken to my parents in a long time. We're…estranged."

A tension filled Mason's chest. He rubbed at a spot, trying to take away the tightness.

He didn't know what else to say because he couldn't imagine that. His parents were healthy and supported him completely. He visited them when he could, and vice versa.

Mason might only call them once a week, but they kept in touch via TVT—the next best thing to being together.

Mason, however, knew others who weren't as fortunate as him.

Brett Matthews's dad had taken off before he was born. His wife, Laurel's dad, had deserted his family to run off with a younger woman and took what was left of their family fortune with him. Questions demanded to be asked, but this wasn't an inquisition. Mason needed to take his time. "I'm sorry."

"Thanks." She sounded resigned, not bitter or sad. "It's for the best."

"Still sucks."

Rachael nodded. "Want to know why?"

"Yes." Not wanting to butt in and be rude had kept him from asking. "But only if you want to tell me."

Something clanged. A group sang "Happy Birthday." A busboy cleared a nearby table.

She closed her eyes and opened them. "My dad is addicted to gambling."

Once again, her words were unexpected. Mason had said he was sorry. He didn't want the words to seem trite, even though he was sad she experienced something so negative in her life.

He covered her hand with his.

"We tried every kind of treatment, but it never helped for long. My mother enabled him—she still does, which made our life seem as if we lived inside a Yo-Yo. Up-down, feast-famine, at times. After I left for college, I decided not to return home unless things changed. They haven't."

"Must get lonely."

She shrugged. "I work holidays. The only time my parents contact me is if they need money. No one in Portland knows about my dad. I'm not even sure why I'm telling you this."

The shame in her voice cut deep. Mason wanted to make her feel better. He squeezed her hand. "It's because I'm easy to talk to. I invented the best communication tool on the internet."

That made her laugh.

Score. But it was time to get serious.

"I also care about you." His affection for her kept increasing. "Your father's disease isn't on you. It hurt you, and you had to protect yourself. Nothing wrong with that."

Gratitude shone in her gaze. "Thank you."

"It's the truth." He wanted her to see what he did. "You're special, Rachael. You run your own event planning company. You're self-made. Like me."

Rachael sat taller. "I am, aren't I?"

He laced his fingers with hers, never wanting to let go. "And trust me, you're going to go far."

Her eyes remained locked on his. "That's the plan."

"It's a good one." And he had plans for tonight. Those involved a good night kiss.

If he got the chance.

But Mason had the feeling he would, and he couldn't wait.

* * *

Rachael wished the dinner didn't have to end, but the restaurant's staff kept side-eyeing them. "I think the place is ready to close."

He glanced at the time. His eyes widened. "I hadn't realized it was this late."

"Me, either. We're the last ones here."

Mason pulled out a money clip from his pocket and tossed a few hundred-dollar bills onto the table. "This will make them feel less put out."

Shock reverberated through her. Until she remembered—billionaire. A hundred dollars was a lot for her. She had to think twice before spending that much on anything. But to Mason, it was nothing.

Good for him.

Tonight, she'd learned he came from a solidly middle-class background. But he enjoyed buying things and spending money, so he did. He wasn't trying to show off or make others jealous. It made him happy.

"If it doesn't make them feel less put out," she teased, "they have a bigger problem than working late."

Rachael stood, and so did he. It had been warm earlier, and she hadn't worn a coat.

She placed the purse strap on her shoulder. "This has been fun."

He nodded, resting his hand at the small of her back.

His touch made her feel special. Everything about tonight had, but especially Mason.

And then she remembered. "We never discussed your dinner."

"How about we do that tomorrow night?" he asked.

A thrill shot through her. "If it's after seven, I can do that."

He opened the door for her. "Later works better for me."

Rachael walked outside. The temperature had dropped, but not that much. She inhaled. The cool air refreshed her. "I'm parked down the street."

"I'll walk you there."

She was about to say no, that it wasn't far, but she wanted to spend as much time with Mason as she could. "Thanks."

As he lowered his arm, she ignored the twinge of disappointment. He held her hand, and all was right in her world. Never in a million years would she have ever thought about dating Mason, but something about him touched her heart. She wanted to see what that was.

Walking in silence was comfortable. The only sounds were car engines, tires against asphalt, and an occasional blast of music from a vehicle passing.

"My car is up ahead. The white hatchback." She spoke with more confidence than she felt. She'd purchased the car used. It was nothing fancy but had an excellent safety rating and room to carry items she needed for an event. "Thanks again for dinner."

"I enjoyed it." He stopped next to her car. "And you."

She smiled at him, unsure what came next. Dates usually

ended in kisses, right?

Rachael wet her lips.

"May I kiss you good night?" he asked.

Not trusting her voice, she nodded.

He lowered his mouth to hers slowly as if giving her time to change her mind, but she was all-in and met him halfway, pressing her lips against his.

Tender.

His kiss was tender and soft and sweet and tasted like chocolate. It must be the dessert they'd shared. She wanted more.

Rachael wasn't sure who increased the pressure, but it happened. His arms wrapped around her. And hers went around Mason.

His kiss filled her up, making her feel invincible.

This was what she dreamed about finding someday. And here it was.

Here *he* was.

Rachael was falling hard and fast, but she didn't care. Mason wasn't like other guys. He was nothing like her father. She had no idea how she knew, but she did. He was worth the risk.

Slowly, Mason drew away from her. It was dark, but a streetlamp showed his wide pupils and quickened breaths.

Did his lips tingle like hers?

He rested his forehead against hers. "I'm looking forward to seeing you tomorrow."

"Me, too." She wiggled her toes.

That was better than touching her lips and spinning

around, which was what she wanted to do. She would do that when she got to her apartment.

She unlocked her car, and he opened the door.

"Drive safe." He kissed her forehead. "And sleep well."

"I will." Rachael also had a feeling her dreams would be sweet tonight. "You, too."

She slid into the driver's seat, forcing herself not to look at him.

The sooner she went to sleep and woke up, the sooner they would be together again. She couldn't wait.

Chapter Seven

One day ran into another. Rachael couldn't believe Mason wanted to spend so much time together, but it had been over a week now, and things were going well. On Saturday afternoon, as she entered the coffee shop where she'd met with Mason, she kept pinching herself.

It had to be a dream.

Except she was wide awake and not in bed.

She sat at a table where she could see the door. She'd wanted to take her business to the next level, and she was on her way. Thanks to Mason, she was now planning his friend Kieran O'Neal's wedding to Selah Burton, who worked for Mason.

Rachael fought the urge to squeal.

Who could blame her?

Mason was a dream come true. Not only for bringing her more events to plan. He understood about her hours. The way she did his. They saw each other as often as they could, and not only to discuss his upcoming event. They'd gone out to dinners, watched movies, and walked hand-in-hand on the path alongside the Willamette River.

A text notification buzzed.

Mason: *See you later?*
Rachael: *I'm meeting with Kieran and Selah in a few minutes, but I'm free after.*
Mason: *Text me when you're finished.*
Rachael: *Will do!*

As anticipation surged, Rachael wiggled her toes. She was falling in love with him. It was fast, but she couldn't stop herself. The truth was, she didn't want to.

A couple walked in, and she recognized the man who'd caught the garter at Adam and Cambria's wedding. She stood and met them halfway. "I'm Rachael Sanders."

"I'm Kieran, and this is my fiancée, Selah."

The pretty woman grinned. "I love hearing you call me that."

"And I love you." He kissed her forehead.

The two were so sweet. Would Rachael and Mason ever be all lovey-dovey like that? Time would tell, but she had a feeling they would be there soon. "I have a table in the corner. Tell me what you'd like to drink, and I'll order it."

"Iced coffee for me," Selah said.

"Make that two."

"That'll be easy to remember." Rachael noticed their linked hands. The two were adorable together. "It shouldn't take long."

A few minutes later, she sat at the table across from the

couple. Kieran had his arm around Selah, who stared up at him as if he'd hung the moon.

"The drinks will be ready shortly." Rachael readied her notebook and pen. "Congratulations on your engagement."

"Thank you," they said in unison.

Too cute. "Why don't you tell me what kind of wedding you'd like? By that, I mean indoors, outside? Formal, rustic? And if you don't know yet, I'd love to know any ideas or things that appeal to you."

"Outside," the couple said at the same time.

"At least a hundred guests." Selah tilted her head. "One hundred twenty-seven if everyone says yes."

Kieran smoothed Selah's hair. "And we want to get married on August seventeenth."

A good thing Rachael didn't have a mouth full of tea, or she would have spewed it all over her new clients or choked. That date was so soon. She inhaled, calming herself before she broke out in a full-on panic and sweat. She'd arranged Adam and Cambria's wedding in less time. Rachael could do this.

"We're off to a great start." Her voice remained steady when her insides trembled. She wrote the date in her notebook along with the guest count. "What else?"

An hour later, Rachael had taken pages of notes. The couple had a solid idea of what they wanted. The trick would be to find the right location given the short timeframe.

"This all seems doable." She scanned her notes. "My biggest concern is the venue. Most of the premium wedding locations book up months in advance."

"We're not giving you much time, but you did a lovely job at Adam and Cambria's wedding," Kieran said. "If we can't find a place, we can use Henry Davenport's estate in Dunthorpe. He owes me."

Selah leaned into him. "You mean us."

"Yes, us." He kissed her head. "I really should make Henry and Mason pay for the wedding given the trouble they caused, but because we're together now, I can let it slide."

Mason? Rachael straightened. Kieran must mean her Mason. Asking outright might be rude, but curiosity got the best of her. "I hope everything is okay."

"It's fine now." Kieran rubbed Selah's diamond engagement ring with his free hand. "But my friends came up with a crazy scheme for me to get to know Selah better. I simply wanted to ask her to dinner, but they told me to pretend I needed help with a project. I didn't like being dishonest about a fake project, but Mason thought it was a fool-proof way to go because it was working for him."

Rachael's insides froze. She gripped her pen so tightly she almost broke it. Mason couldn't mean her. But if not her, who? Was he dating someone else? They'd never agreed to be exclusive, but…

Selah lowered her iced coffee. "How we ended up together doesn't matter. But I think both Mason and Henry learned their lesson."

Maybe not.

"I'm glad it worked out." Rachael forced the words out because she had to say something.

Selah beamed. "Us, too."

Kieran nodded. "It was touch and go for a few days."

Selah nodded.

Rachael's hand shook. "I have what I need to get started. I'll reach out tomorrow night. I'd like to meet again this week, if possible."

"That's fine," Selah said. "I'm on a leave of absence from work."

Kieran kissed her hand. "You don't have to go back."

Selah shrugged. "I'm enjoying not working more than I thought I would, but returning to TVT might be the only way to stop Mason from sending me flowers every day."

"It's a boon for local florists." Kieran laughed.

"That's one way to look at it," Selah said.

Kieran winked. "Groveling is another."

Rachael was missing something—something big—but it had only been Mason and her. He'd mentioned his friends in passing. These two didn't seem to know he was dating her.

She placed her notebook and pen in her purse. She'd barely touched her iced tea, but that usually happened when she met clients. "I'll be in touch tomorrow."

Tonight, she would talk to Mason and find out what was going on.

* * *

Mason wasn't much of a cook. He'd picked up takeout on his way home from work. He'd spent all day Saturday there with one thing on his mind—seeing Rachael later. She'd texted she was on her way.

After he placed the food in the oven to keep warm, he rubbed his hands together. His plan was working.

She was planning two events thanks to him—his dinner and Kieran's wedding. Soon, she'd have so much work she could pick what events she wanted to do.

A knock sounded.

Eager to see her, he hurried to the front door and opened it.

Rachael stood on his porch, but she wasn't smiling.

His chest tightened. He didn't like seeing her upset. "Come in."

She did, and he closed the door.

"How did the meeting with Kieran and Selah go?" he asked.

"Great, but…"

As Mason reached toward her, she stepped away.

"They mentioned your and Henry's part in their relationship."

Mason's stomach dropped. "I—"

"Kieran said you'd done something similar to what you told him to do." Rachael's voice sharpened. "Is that why you asked me to plan a dinner party?"

Mason swore. Kieran had said to come clean before it was too late. "We're different."

"How?"

Once she understood Mason's reasoning, she would be fine with what had happened. Things were too good between them for her to walk away. "Well, I asked you out on a date for coffee, but you thought it was a business meeting. I figured why not have you plan an event for me. I could get to know you better and introduce your business to my friends and acquaintances. A win-win."

"That's—"

"Two birds, brilliant."

"Dishonest," she said a beat later. "I thought my work at Adam and Cambria's wedding impressed you."

Her accusatory tone told Mason he had some work to do. "It did. You, however, impressed me more. I didn't lie about wanting to have a dinner party, but it was a spur-of-the-moment event."

Her gaze narrowed. "Like a fake project?"

"I wanted to spend time with you."

"At your whim."

"That's not fair."

She crossed her arms over her chest. "I trusted you."

"You still can."

"I can't." Rachael stepped away from him. "How will I know this isn't only a game to you? That you won't tire of me?"

"It's not like that." Mason moved closer, only to have her step away. He needed her to understand how he felt about her. "I care about you."

Her lower lip quivered. "Not enough to tell me the truth."

"I was going to."

She raised her chin. "When?"

"Soon."

"Not soon enough." Rachael pulled out a folder from

her bag and handed him pieces of paper. "Everything is on track for your dinner. I emailed you the contracts, but here are printouts if you like hard copies. If you have questions, please let me know. Otherwise, I'll be in touch for the final headcount."

He felt as if he'd been sucker-punched. "That sounds like a goodbye."

She lifted her chin a notch. "It is."

"I'm sorry." Mason's voice cracked. "I made a mistake."

"You made two." Her words shot out like arrows striking his heart. "You saw what you did to Selah and Kieran, yet that didn't make you rethink what you were doing with me."

Mason had billions he would spend on whatever it took to make this up to Rachael. "I told you we're different."

"Except we're not." She inhaled deeply, and her eyes gleamed. "Trusting anyone is hard for me, but I trusted you about my family. I may not be a Billionaire of Silicon Forest or make six-figures, but I deserve better from the man I fell in love with."

His mouth went dry. Rachael loved him?

She half laughed. "Silly me thought I was in love with you when this was only an amusing charade for you. Something to keep you from being bored. A fun story to tell your friends over cocktails and caviar."

"Rachael—"

"I grew up a little like Henry Davenport. We had a chauffeur and a house staff. Until my dad lost it all, but that wasn't the worst part. It was the lies. About him getting help.

About him wanting to change. About him not gambling. He lied to my mom and me. And continued to lie. He's still lying."

"I didn't mean to hurt you." The words tumbled from Mason's mouth. She had to know how he felt. "I want to be with you."

"I wanted to be with you, too, but now… You hurt me. And I have no idea who Mason Reese really is."

Before he could say anything, she walked out of his house, leaving him with only the paperwork for his dinner party.

Go after her.

His heart lodged in his throat. And his eyelids burned.

Mason's gut told him to show her who he really was. He wasn't the man she believed him to be. But his feet remained glued to the entryway.

He wanted to go after her, but what would he say?

Because a part of him knew she was right. From the moment he'd met her, he was no longer sure who Mason Reese was.

Chapter Eight

The three weeks passed in a blur for Rachael. Somehow—with a huge hat tip to Henry Davenport—she'd pulled off Kieran and Selah's wedding. It had been a mad rush, but that had given Rachael less time to think about…

Not now.

Keep yourself together and in control. That's what the bride and groom deserve. Besides, it would only be a few more hours until the reception ended.

After the serving staff cleaned up the dessert plates, Rachael made a pass around the tent to see if she needed to take care of anything. The temperature was a balmy eighty on this warm August night. Still, the tent—decorated with fabric, chandeliers, and garlands of fresh flowers—stayed cool thanks to discrete and quiet portable air conditioning units. Henry had gone overboard with the fairy lights on the trees and shrubs in his backyard, but the effect was whimsical, magical, and oh-so-romantic. The bride and groom had thanked Rachael for everything, and she'd passed on the praise to Henry, who'd beamed like a kid in a toy store.

As couples, including Selah and Kieran, danced to live music, Rachael removed the schedule from her jacket pocket. She only had two skirts with matching jackets that were nice enough to wear for fancier events. The first she'd worn for Cambria and Adam's wedding. The other tonight. Mason hadn't canceled his event at the winery yet, but she assumed he would, and that would keep her from having to buy a new outfit to wear.

Mason.

A heaviness weighed her down, making it difficult to breathe.

Stop.

A high-profile, bespoke wedding wasn't the time or place to be sad and brokenhearted. Business came first. Besides, they'd been civil, exchanging pleasantries earlier since he was the best man. After that, she'd kept her distance, and he hadn't sought her out.

A win-win, as he would say.

If only doing that had been as easy as she made it sound because seeing Mason in yet another tuxedo took her back to the night they'd met at Cambria and Adam's wedding. That had only been five weeks ago, but it seemed as if a lifetime had passed.

Part of her missed Mason. The other part flipped between anger and confusion, depending on the hour. But she would get over it.

Him.

Someday.

All she had to do was survive the rest of the reception.

With her resolve in place, Rachael checked the schedule. The bouquet and garter toss were up next. Not all couples included those—anniversary dances had become a popular alternative—but Kieran had been adamant about the garter toss since he'd caught it at the last wedding. Selah agreed, even though she'd told him wedding traditions didn't always play out in reality. He remained undeterred.

Rachael tucked the list into her pocket.

"You outdid yourself once again." Henry came up to her. It was the first time all night he didn't have a glass of champagne in hand. "My backyard has never looked as romantic and beautiful. If someone hadn't gotten married tonight, it would be the perfect spot for a proposal. Your hard work paid off."

"Thanks, but I had lots of help between the florists, caterers, and you. Your staff did an amazing job with all the lights. Thanks for letting us hold the wedding and reception here." Rachael had only slept a few hours a night this week, but seeing the bride's awe and the groom's relief had been worth the exhaustion. "I also appreciate you letting me stay in your guest cottage. It made working here so much easier."

"My pleasure." Henry's lips parted. "I have a brilliant idea. The place is usually empty, so you should move in."

She startled. His matter-of-fact tone made the suggestion sound almost normal. Except it wasn't. Typical of the generous billionaire, but not what she was used to. "Why would you want me to do that?"

"I know where you live. This is safer."

"It's not the best area, but it's okay."

"Independent. I forgot." Henry blew out a breath. "I'll charge whatever rent you pay now if that makes you feel better. The money will be donated to charity. Or don't pay me. Either way, the offer is genuine."

Billionaires lived in a different galaxy than everyone else. She would love to live on the palatial estate a few miles south of downtown Portland in a luxurious guest house, but something held her back.

Okay, someone.

"That's such a generous offer. I love staying at the guest cottage, but I can't move in." She forced the words from her dry throat, even though she would have loved saying yes instead.

But what else could she do?

Henry and Mason were close friends. Rachael wasn't ready to bump into him regularly or see him with another woman. She swallowed around the lump in her throat.

"Don't say no yet," Henry urged. "Think about it, please."

She nodded. But only because he'd saved her a massive headache by letting them use his estate today. Every other place had been booked.

Henry winked. "A glass of champagne has my name on it. I'll talk with you later."

He took off toward one of the bars, even though servers passed out drinks.

A few minutes later, Selah and Kieran left the dance floor.

As the two came up to Rachael, Selah held her husband's

hand. "You look like you need us to do something."

Rachael nodded. "After this, the only thing left is when you leave. We have sparklers for people to hold, so there is some timing involved."

Selah shimmied her shoulders. "The wedding and reception have been positively dreamy and so much better than I imagined it being given the short timeframe."

Kieran raised their linked hands to his mouth and kissed his wife's hand. "We can't thank you enough. This place, the food, everything has been amazing. You're a miracle worker, Rachael."

Not really. She simply had worked hard, but she appreciated the compliment. "Thank you."

A piano player made eye contact with Rachael and handed her the toss bouquet from a vase on his piano.

"Are you ready?" she asked the bride and the groom.

Both nodded.

Rachael gave the signal to the two piano players.

"It's time for the bridal toss," one of the piano players said into his microphone. "Will all the single ladies please come out on the dance floor?"

Rachael handed the bouquet to the bride and positioned herself on the stage. Kieran stared at his bride with such love Rachael's chest hurt.

Selah raised the flowers. "Who wants it?"

The women on the dance floor held up their hands or shouted, "Me!"

"When you're ready, turn around," Rachael whispered, even though they'd gone over this before. Better safe than sorry. "One of the piano players will do the countdown."

As Selah turned away from the crowd, two women pushed their way to the front of the crowd.

"On three," the pianist said. "One, two, three…"

Selah tossed it over her shoulder. The flowers flew.

A red-headed woman caught it and held up the bouquet. "Finally!"

People laughed.

"Now, it's the gentlemen's time," the other piano player said into his mic. "All single men out on the dance floor."

Other men came out there, but Rachael's gaze zeroed in on the four single billionaires of Silicon Forest. Wes and Dash didn't hesitate, and Blaise trudged forward. Mason appeared resigned. Henry followed them, but he stopped on the edge of the wood floor. He held champagne flutes in both hands.

Kieran grinned at his friends before turning away from the men.

"On three," the second pianist said. "One, two, three…"

The lacy garter flew toward Wes until it curved and hit Mason's chest. He grabbed the wisp of lingerie before it hit the ground.

People cheered.

Henry raised both glasses in the air. "Looks like we know who the next groom will be. I wonder what kind of wedding Rachael will plan for you and your bride."

Rachael's heart sank. She'd never turned down an event if a date was free but forget about being professional. She wouldn't be able to plan Mason's wedding. Not even if it were years away.

Kieran gave Mason a thumbs up.

Selah laughed before shaking her head.

Rachael's gaze met Mason's. Her heart slammed against her rib cage, and she focused on the bride and groom. "It's time for pictures with the people who caught the bouquet and garter."

She stepped away, wanting to put distance between her and Mason. Part of her wanted to retreat to the other side of the tent, but she needed to make sure the reception stayed on schedule.

The photographer positioned the four people. She took pictures of the women and the men, and she told them to dance so that he could take more photographs.

As Mason and the woman with the bouquet slow-danced, he said something, and she laughed.

Rachael's stomach burned. She clenched her teeth until her jaw hurt.

Look away.

She did.

It wasn't as if she was required to be there now. Soon, the bride and groom would leave while guests held sparklers. She'd better make sure everything was ready for the newlyweds' departure.

Anything would be better than watching Mason, who seemed happy to dance with someone else. Of course, he was. She meant nothing to him.

Out of sight, out of mind.
Rachael hoped that worked with Mason.
And with her.

***

As the caterers left the reception, Mason returned to the backyard. He had drunk nothing since he caught the garter. It was in his pocket, but the thing might as well be dangling on a stick in front of his face.

He'd been waiting for the festivities to end so that he could speak with Rachael.

All his money wouldn't help his cause. If anything, that would hurt him.

But he had a plan.

Well, his heart did.

Odds were he would crash and burn in a spectacular fiery ball of flames. But that wouldn't be worse than the misery of the past three weeks. That and the glimmer of hope he would succeed made it worth trying. At this point, he had nothing to lose.

He brushed his fingertips over the silk and lace garter.

For luck.

The once-full tent was now empty. The white lights in the trees lit up the backyard, making him feel like he were in a theme park. He nearly laughed because having Henry in his life was a roller coaster ride.

Mason followed the stone pathway toward the guest cottage. It resembled something out of a fairy tale. Laurel

Matthews—nee Worthington—had stayed there before she and Brett reunited.

Lights were on inside.

Good. Rachael must be tired, but Mason would have woken her. He didn't want to wait any longer.

He knocked.

No answer.

Mason knocked again.

The door opened slowly. Rachael wore a robe. Her hair was wet. "Mason?"

He shoved his fingertips into his pockets. "Hi."

Not the strongest opening, but she hadn't slammed the door in his face. He'd take that as a win.

Her eyebrows drew together, causing two lines to form above the bridge of her nose. That always happened when she was thinking about something.

Rachael's mouth slanted. "What are you doing here?"

"I want to talk to you." He rocked back on his heels. "You were busy with the wedding earlier."

"I just got out of the shower." Her hand remained on the knob. "I'm tired."

"You worked hard. Selah and Kieran thought everything was perfect, and it was. Thanks to you." The words poured from Mason's lips like snow runoff over Multnomah Falls. He couldn't stop. If he did, she might tell him to leave. "I only need a few minutes."

She stared at the welcome mat he stood on.

"Please." If he had to beg, so be it.

Rachael tightened the belt around her robe. "A few minutes."

Relief rushed through him. "Thank you."

She stepped away from the doorway.

Mason walked inside, afraid if he hesitated, she would change her mind. "I'm sorry."

As Rachael flinched, her eyes widened.

"You were right. I was wrong." Admitting that was easier than he thought it would be. "I went about everything wrong. I wanted to be smart about you, but I was an idiot. I hurt you, which was the last thing I wanted to happen. I can't change the past, but I will do better in the future…with you."

Her forehead wrinkled. "Me?"

He nodded, taking a step toward her. "You're the one for me. My heart recognized it the night of Cambria and Adam's wedding, but my mind took a while to catch up. Today, when Selah and Kieran exchanged vows, I knew that's what I wanted…with you. Marry me."

She gasped.

"I know we're not dating right now, and I take full responsibility for that." He took a breath. "But we're perfect for each other. Not that either of us is perfect. But you're my perfect woman. So, there's no reason not to dive into the deep end. When you know, you know, and now that I know, I don't want to wait to be with you. These past three weeks have been hard enough. So will you marry me?"

Her mouth gaped. "I need a minute to digest everything you've said."

Mason opened his mouth before pressing his lips together.

Quiet. He needed to be quiet.

His neck itched. Or was it his shoulder? A game show

countdown song played in his head. He ignored both, not wanting to fidget.

Mason remembered he'd forgotten the most important thing.

How could he have said all the other stuff but not…that?

She'd wanted him not to talk, so he raised his hand.

The two lines deepened. "What?"

"I love you."

Rachael's lips parted. "You…"

"I love you." He relished the way the words sounded. He wanted to keep repeating it for the next sixty or seventy years, but now wasn't the time to tell her that.

Her eyes gleamed.

His heart dropped. "This is too much for you. You're tired. Go to bed. We can talk tomorrow. Or the next day. Whenever you're free. I'll—"

"I accept your apology." She rose up and kissed him softly on the lips. "I love you."

His lips tingled, and his heart pounded.

She left him dazed but happy. So very happy.

This was going better than he expected.

"You've dropped a lot on me," she said.

Now wasn't the time to get antsy and push her, even though he wanted to do that.

Mason nodded. "You can think everything over, and you haven't said yes to my proposal, but there's one more thing you need to consider."

"What?"

He took a breath. "Any chance you could turn my dinner party at the winery into our wedding and reception?"

Epilogue

September

As the groom slid the garter from the bride's leg, guests cheered. Blaise Mortenson didn't join in. Instead, he rubbed the back of his neck and tried not to frown. A multimillion-dollar wedding at a winery in Oregon's Willamette Valley with performances by singers who graced the top of the Billboard charts and dinner prepared by a Michelin-star chef, yet the newlyweds had included every reception tradition pinned on Pinterest.

Given the bride was a successful event planner, he shouldn't be surprised. The groom's two-point-six-billion-dollar net worth meant everything tonight was over-the-top bespoke.

Blaise fought the urge to step outside and check his email. Better yet, to return to his hotel room and his laptop.

But he couldn't.

His friends would never let him hear the end of it. And rightly so. Tonight was worth celebrating.

Three down, two to go.

Mason Reese saying "I do" today meant the social media app billionaire was out. He'd lost the bet. Surprising—okay, shocking—because he'd come up with the "last single man standing" wager five years ago.

Half of the six friends who took part were now married. All within the past three months. Which was why, as soon as Mason announced his engagement and wedding date, Blaise had stopped drinking the tap water in the Portland metro area.

Crazy, yes, but he wasn't taking any chances. He even brushed his teeth with bottled water. Call him superstitious or paranoid, but something in the water would explain why his friends were falling in love and marrying so fast. Not that Blaise minded the rash of nuptials or having to purchase each couple a wedding gift.

Only two more to go until he won the bet.

He would be the last single man standing no matter what it took.

Losing wasn't an option.

A drum roll played.

"Are all the single men on the dance floor?" a singer who had recently finished a world tour asked with a grating voice. As she glanced around, her eyes, caked with thick eyeliner and heavy mascara, lingered on Blaise Mortenson before doing the same to Wes and Dash.

Blaise's muscles tightened.

Typical.

Except most women only saw their net worth. Much of

which was tied up in their respective companies or funds, in his case, but the term billionaire implied an extravagant lifestyle, one with an American Express "Black" card and a Visa "White" card. Few understood the work involved in running a successful company. The attention from gorgeous women used to be flattering to Blaise, who'd been bullied in school, a nerd who girls ignored. Now, he found most women who wanted to date him vapid—the definition of annoying.

The singer glanced at the groom, who grinned like a cat waiting for a second serving of canary. "Are you ready?"

Ready for another drink—a shot.

Tequila or whiskey, Blaise didn't care with the top-shelf liquor being poured by generous bartenders. A famous mixologist had been flown in from New York to create signature wedding cocktails.

Other men, however, whooped and hollered as if the outcome of their evening depended on catching the bride's garter.

Losers.

But they were welcome to it.

"Smiling won't kill you, Mortenson," Wes teased. "Wedding receptions are supposed to be fun."

"I was having fun until you made me come out here."

Even if Blaise wanted to argue about being forced to participate, he wouldn't. A few of his company's board of directors were here somewhere. They'd been on him about being nicer to his employees. Besides, Mason and his bride deserved better than Blaise causing a scene.

To appease Wes, Blaise forced the corners of his mouth upward in a move he'd perfected.

"Three, two, one…" the singer said into the microphone.

Mason shot the blue and white garter. It soared through the air on a direct trajectory toward…

Blaise cursed under his breath. His tuxedo-clad shoulders sagged.

This had to be a setup.

Too bad, because he wasn't playing.

He shoved the tips of his fingers into his pockets.

The garter hit his left lapel before dropping to the floor.

People gasped.

A few laughed.

Another snickered.

The drummer hit the cymbal.

He ignored them. Otherwise, he might be tempted to scoop up the blue silk and lace-trimmed garter lying across the toe of his patent-leather derby shoe.

Focus on winning the bet.

About the Author

USA Today bestselling author Melissa McClone has written over forty-five sweet contemporary romance novels. She lives in the Pacific Northwest with her husband, three children, a spoiled Norwegian Elkhound, and cats who think they rule the house. They do!

If you'd like to find Melissa online:

Website
www.melissamcclone.com

Facebook
www.facebook.com/melissamcclonebooks

McClone Troopers Reader Facebook Group
www.facebook.com/groups/McCloneTroopers

Twitter
@melissamcclone

Instagram
@melmcclone

Other Books by Melissa Mcclone

The Billionaires of Silicon Forest
Who will be the last single man standing?
The Gold Digger
The Kiss Catcher
The Game Changer
The Wife Finder
The Wish Maker
The Deal Breaker

One Night to Forever Series
Can one night change your life…and your relationship status?
Fiancé for the Night
The Wedding Lullaby
A Little Bit Engaged
Love on the Slopes
The One Night To Forever Box Set: Books 1-4

Mountain Rescue Series
Finding love in Hood Hamlet with a
little help from Christmas magic…
His Christmas Wish
Her Christmas Secret
Her Christmas Kiss
His Second Chance
His Christmas Family

The Beach Brides/Indigo Bay Miniseries
Prequels to the Berry Lake Cupcake Posse series…
Jenny (Jenny and Dare)
Sweet Holiday Wishes (Lizzy and Mitch)
Sweet Beginnings (Hope and Josh)
Sweet Do-Over (Marley and Von)

Sweet Yuletide (Sheridan and Michael)

The Berry Lake Cupcake Posse Series
Can five friends save their small town's beloved bakery?
Cupcakes & Crumbs
Tiaras & Teacups
Kittens & Kisses

Her Royal Duty
Royal romances with charming princes and dreamy castles...
The Reluctant Princess
The Not-So-Proper Princess
The Proper Princess

Quinn Valley Ranch
Two books featuring siblings in a multi-author series...
Carter's Cowgirl
Summer Serenade
Quinn Valley Ranch Two Book Set

A Keeper Series
These men know what they want, and love isn't on their list.
But what happens when each meets a keeper?
The Groom
The Soccer Star
The Boss
The Husband
The Date
The Tycoon

For the complete list of books, go to:
melissamcclone.com/books.com

www.ingramcontent.com/pod-product-compliance
Lightning Source LLC
Chambersburg PA
CBHW050833190726
48286CB00007B/2072